Sorrow's Heart

G. S. Scott

True Tree Press

PO BOX 81168

Lansing, MI 48908

Sorrow's Heart

A True Tree Chronicles Story

Cover by Colleen Nye

Cover Image by Vargazs

Editing by Melissa Ringsted and There For You Editing

Formatting by Colleen Nye

Author photo by Rita Deibler

Published by: True Tree Press

PO BOX 81168 Lansing, MI 48908

TrueTreePress@gmail.com

Copyright © 2015, 2016, 2018 True Tree Press & G. S. Scott
Printed in the United States of America
Third printing

All rights reserved.

No part of this book may be reproduced or transmitted in any form or by any means, electronic or mechanical, including photocopying, recording or by any information storage and retrieval system, without written permission from the publisher.

The unauthorized reproduction or distribution of a copyrighted work is illegal. Criminal copyright infringement, including infringement without monetary gain, is investigated by the FBI and is punishable by fines and federal imprisonment.

This is a work of fiction. All characters and situations appearing in this work are fictitious. Any resemblance to real persons, living or dead, or personal situations is purely coincidental.

For Sarah

Chapters:

Chapter 1 – Chattel – pg. 3

Chapter 2 – Abatement – 15

Chapter 3 – Rekindling – pg. 35

Chapter 4 – The Lord's Blessing – pg. 49

Chapter 5 – Jasper – pg. 63

Chapter 6 – Violation – pg. 81

Chapter 7 – Presentable – pg. 95

Chapter 8 – The Dinner – pg. 107

Chapter 9 – Casandra – pg. 127

Chapter 10 – Tears – pg. 147

The True Tree Chronicles:

I am the True Tree.

The Mother of all.

I am the wellspring from which all life flows.

From my branches and roots, come the seeds and pods of all forms of life.

Wherever there is life, I am there.

Wherever there is death, I am there.

Life and death are one.

What is returned to me in death shall be brought forth once more into life.

I am the mighty.

I am the meek.

I am the one.

I, am singular.

I, am True.

.

Chapter 1

Chattel

The Girl's naked skin soaked up the sunlight as she gazed out the window, temporarily washing away the ever-present ache in her back and rawness of her fingers. She lazily polished the oaken console table, being careful not to overturn the brass lamp at its edge. The sun shone through a myriad of light dancing clouds, and the thick trees swayed in the breeze and birds flitted from limb to limb.

It was a beautiful day, but she knew it wouldn't last. In a world under the influence of the Lord God of Chaos, the weather changed as often as did the Lord himself.

The day's light poured through the multitude of windows of the massive library filled with a hodgepodge of shelves, all stuffed with books and scrolls. It illuminated dust motes that danced in the air and bathing the room with its glow. The smell of the beeswax in the polish intermingled with the lamp oil, and the ash from the two massive unlit fireplaces at either end, gave the room a pleasant atmosphere.

The Girl often felt her smallest while standing in that enormous room; a lonely, insignificant speck in a world she hated.

A sudden swirl of clouds obscured the sun, causing her to shudder with the sudden chill. Like the rest of the Master's children, she wore no clothing. Clothing cost money and since they never went outside Master Ruddick decided they didn't need any.

The brisk air shook her out of her introspection. She hastened on to the other tables in the library, cursing herself for staring out the window in the first place. It wasn't as though she were going anywhere.

He allowed the children out of their cages for only a short time. And in that time they needed to muck out their cages, as well as those of the animals, and place it all in the refuse room at the top of the stairs where the stableman would dispose of it outside. They also had to clean two rooms each. She had the two largest rooms in the mansion that day. A common occurrence.

After completing the rest of her dusting and sweeping, she ran for the kitchen. Her bare feet, slapping on the wooden floor, echoed down the mostly empty hall. Bursting through the kitchen door, she skidded to a halt and took her food tray from the smiling cook, Dorinda, before heading to her cage in the basement.

The backdoor to the stable yard stood open allowing the cool day's air to flow in, filled with a heady mixture of the smells of the stables, exercise green, and the forest beyond. As she passed by she caught sight of the stableman, Kos, exercising one of the horses. When he looked up from his work and saw her watching him with the horse, he smiled wickedly. She felt her nudity most when the stableman leered at her like that.

She turned away from the stable yard door, rushed past the refuse room and to the stone stairs to the basement where she, along with another dozen children, lived. She did her best to keep her wooden tray of steaming hot food as still as possible. Master Ruddick might not want to spend money on clothing his children but he fed them well and grew quite angry if any of it went to waste.

The stone steps were ice cold beneath her feet as she descended. The ever-present sounds of the animals that also resided in the basement, along with the smells of mold, mildew, shit and piss funneled up at her.

Once she reached the bottom of the stairs, she raced down the short hallway to the massive open basement. There, Master Ruddick waited for her at the door to her cage. His long black hair, hanging loose about his shoulders, waved as he shook his head at seeing her. She was the last to arrive.

"Hurry up," he barked. "I haven't got all day."

She scurried into the cage she shared with Rosh and two other boys, Erik and Nash. He slammed the cage door behind her, nearly catching her heel, and snapped on the lock.

Then without another word he turned and made his way to one of the animal pens at the back of the basement, his silk slippers and gray robes barely making a sound.

"Took you long enough," Rosh said with a sneer and grabbed one of her two buttered rolls from her tray before she made her way to her usual spot at the front corner of the cage.

Once seated, she ate quickly while the others, having already finished their meal, stared at her. She reveled in the succulence of the chicken, moist and heartily spiced, as well as the vegetables, a mixture of beans and broccoli with a light coating of salt. She also had a small wedge of cheese that held a sharp bite, offsetting her ewe's milk.

Before she could finish, Eric rushed forward and grabbed her second roll, but he didn't get to keep it. Rosh grabbed him by the arm and flung him to the back of the cage. Eric's head banged on the bars, and then he rebounded, staggering to the center of the cage where Rosh punched him square in the face. The black-haired boy's nose gushed blood, and he fell to the straw and sawdust-covered floor in a heap.

Rosh stared menacingly at Nash, and then swung his attention to the other two cages on the opposite side of the walkway. The children there lowered their eyes. Rosh was by far the oldest and strongest of them, and they had all experienced the brunt of his anger in the past.

She held mixed feelings about Rosh. Deep down she had doubts that he was even her brother, no matter what he claimed. They didn't resemble each other in the least. His hair was a dirty blond, and he had blue eyes, whereas her own eyes and hair were as brown as mud. They didn't even look alike. He often cursed her out and blamed her for their being sold in the first place. Whenever something went wrong, he would abuse her. She hated him for that.

On the other hand, he also protected her from the other children. But that protection caused its own problems. It separated her from the others, leaving Rosh the only one who interacted with her, adding to her isolation. Not that she cared, or so she told herself. She didn't want to get to know any of the others. The children died so often that she stopped trying to make friends long ago. Why befriend someone who would only die, anyway?

The Girl wolfed down her meal, including the roll Rosh retrieved for her, slid the tray through the bars, and lay down to sleep for a bit. There wasn't much to do once they finished their daily chores and meal.

As she drifted off, a pained screech from the back where the Master conducted most his of his experiments startled her. She shuddered and tried to go back to sleep but failed. The animal's painful cries went on for quite some time before coming to a sudden and sharp halt.

She looked up in time to see Master Ruddick toss the animal's bloody body upon the refuse pile. She once heard one of the others call it a 'monkey'. She did her best not to throw up her meal. It was simply another reminder of where her cursed parents had left her.

Master Ruddick was a priest to the Lord of Chaos and he conducted experiments on the animals as well as the children. She had no idea what the old man was doing to any of them. She only knew it hurt.

"What happened here?" the Master asked in his thin voice as he walked toward them. When no one replied he scoffed, "Nothing to say? So be it, animals."

She shook in fear as he scrutinized her. He waved his right hand back and forth several times. The magic struck the Girl, and she sucked in her breath through clenched teeth. She felt as though razors sliced into her skin. Her belly writhed as if filled with maggots, and a fire burned behind her eyes. She convulsed upon the floor of their cage.

He caused the pain not as a punishment; it was a simple part of their routine. He committed his sick experiments on all of them every few days or so. The aftereffects always differed as did the time it took to recover. Sometimes it took only minutes while other times it lasted several hours. She just wished he hadn't done it right after her dinner.

She picked up her head, not knowing how long she had lain there in a pool of her own urine and vomit, and saw she was the first to recover. Nash and her brother lay quivering and crying on the floor. But Eric didn't make a sound.

She crawled over to him and shook him, but to no avail. When she turned his head toward her, she discovered his eyes were dull and vacant. She knew he was dead. It wasn't the first time Master Ruddick had killed one of them with his sorcery. It had happened countless times before.

With a sigh she crawled to Eric's former corner of the cage. She didn't want to return to her own until the sawdust and straw soaked up her discharge. She curled into a ball and refused to cry. She promised herself long ago to never do that again. Tears brought only more pain and did little to soothe her.

A week passed after Eric's death and life went on as normal: more chores, more pain, more isolation. The only change was in Rosh—he'd been less cruel as of late and would often seem dazed and lackadaisical.

She awoke one day by Rosh shaking her out of her stupor caused by yet another of Master Ruddick's spells. Her mind felt thick and her eyesight was hazy. When her sight finally cleared, she looked at Rosh and shrieked at what she saw.

He slapped her in the face. "What the hell's wrong with you?" he yelled. "You've been asleep for almost a day. I just wanted to see if you were still alive."

She stared at Rosh through the tears caused by his slap, wanting to see if her eyes were playing tricks on her. They weren't.

"Your eyes," she stammered. "They're changing color."

"What are you talking about?" He stood. "What game are you playing at?" He kicked her in the ribs. "Huh? You trying to play with my head? Is that it? I'll give you a game," he growled and kicked her several more times.

"No, I swear," she cried out to him. "I'm telling the truth. Tell him, Nash."

"It's true," the boy replied while backing into his own corner. "She's telling the truth. I saw it earlier. I just didn't want to believe it."

Rosh appeared dumbfounded, glancing between the two. "No," he mumbled, shaking his head. "No. No," he screamed and kicked the Girl harder than ever. She curled tightly into a ball, trying to protect herself.

"What's going on back here?" she heard Master Ruddick's voice as he approached. "What are you doing? Stop that!"

The blows ceased, and she heard her brother grunt. She opened her eyes. Rosh was standing stiff and hovering a foot off the floor.

"Answer me, damn it," the Master snapped in a tight voice as he spun Rosh toward him. His eyes widened, and he said with a hint of awe, "What's this? Can it be?" Rosh hovered toward the front of the cage and the Master peered closely at him. "Yes. Yes, it finally worked!"

The Master bent over, removed the lock, and swung open the door. "Come with me, young man," Master Ruddick instructed as he magically hauled her thrashing brother through the door. He closed and re-locked the cage before looking into Rosh's eyes again. "They said it couldn't be done. Come along, young man. I have some experiments I need to run on you if this is to go to a second stage."

Rosh screamed at the top of his lungs as the Master hauled him to the back of the basement.

For three days and nights, they heard Rosh's screams, moans, and cries. And for those three days and nights they all remained locked in their cages. Dorinda came down to give them their food, handing out simple meals of meats, breads, and cheeses of various types. The cook took care of them but she didn't say a word, she just gazed upon them with pity.

On the fourth day it all ended when the Girl awoke to silence. It scared her. Rosh had not returned. She gazed around the basement and gasped. Rosh's body lay atop the refuse pile.

Chapter 2

Abatement

It had been six months since Rosh died and Master Ruddick seemed to double his efforts. The painful spells he cast upon them grew much stronger and came more often. Many more followed her brother onto the refuse pile.

Andik, a recently acquired child from the southeast, spit at the Girl through his dark stained teeth as she entered the kitchen from the basement. He sneered and laughed at her after doing so. It wasn't the first time he'd done it. Since the day the Master acquired him, Andik kicked, punched, pushed, and spit at all the other children in an attempt to prove he was top dog.

The girl just took it in stride.

"I decided that you're doing all my work today," the gangly, tanned boy said.

"No, I'm not," she replied as she headed for the library.

The boy pushed her to the floor, from behind, as she passed. "Did you hear what I said? You're doing all my work. I'm too tired to do it myself."

The night before the Master's spells had taken a lot out of all of them. But the Girl wasn't about to do the work of two people just because some uppity newcomer said so. "I said no," she snapped as she stood, her hands clenched into fists.

He growled and shoved her to the floor once more and kicked her. The kicking quickly stopped, and she heard Andik give out a shriek. The boy tumbled to the floor next to the Girl, writhing in pain.

"I'll have none of this shit," she heard Master Ruddick say from the top of the basement stairs. "Get your little asses to work." He then turned and walked back down into the basement.

He had struck the boy with his priestly powers, which was something he did with alacrity if he felt the children were sloughing off in their work.

The Girl jumped to her feet and looked down at Andik. She simply smiled at the boy as he panted from the painful punishment he'd just received.

The door to the stables opened and Dorinda stopped at seeing the two. "What are you two doing? Get to work before the Master strikes you for your dawdling." She entered the kitchen, leaving the door open to let in the pleasant morning air.

"Too late," the Girl remarked with a sneer.

Andik still lay on the floor, crying, the Girl realized. So much for the little tough boy, she thought. "Come on, little cry-boy," she said to him. "You have work to do."

The boy stared up at her, hate and pain filling his eyes. He glanced back at the cook, then at the open door. The Girl's heart skipped a beat. She knew what was going through his head.

Before she could say a word, Andik jumped to his feet and bolted for the open door. It seemed like he'd had enough and wanted to escape. But no one escaped Master Ruddick's grasp, not ever.

The moment Andik stepped outside he sputtered and gagged, and he fell to the ground. The Girl watched as Andik writhed on the ground, his face turning bright red and his eyes bulged and bled. His heels drummed the ground, and he clawed at his throat, trying to tear away the invisible band that was choking him to death.

The Girl heard the hastened steps of the Master as he ran up the stairs. Once in the kitchen he flung one hand at Andik and the boy levitated off the ground. The Master magically pulled the boy back inside the manor house and set him back on the floor. The boy's breath came in straggled gasps and his neck dripped blood from his clawing at it. When the Master waved his hand over Andik, the boy's breathing returned, albeit raspy.

Master Ruddick turned his gaze to the Girl. She bolted down the hall. She knew about the spells the Master placed upon all the doors and windows, most everyone did, but she'd never seen just what they did. The Girl ran as hard as she could, deathly afraid the Master would cast her outside just to teach her a lesson.

After that day, Andik had an ever present wheeze, and he'd lost his sight. He didn't live long.

As the days passed, more and more children died from the Master's spells. When only eight of them remained, he split them into two of the cages, leaving the third empty. He used to not care which children when into which cage, but that changed as well. He stopped mixing them all about and kept them in two separate groups. The Girl shared her cage with Dak, a dark-haired boy who'd lived there longer than the Girl, a blonde-haired girl named Acey, and Nash.

One day, the Girl noticed Master Ruddick seemed to cast his spells upon the children in the other cage more often. With every passing day those children grew weaker, and one by one they all died.

He acquired new children at a greater pace to replace those who died. She couldn't help but feel pity for them. They had no idea what was coming and quite often they just couldn't take it. A couple of them died the first time Master

Ruddick used his magic on them. A part of the Girl felt they were the lucky ones.

With Master Ruddick's primary focus being on his newly acquired subjects, the Girl and her cagemates had more work to do. Thankfully, it also meant he gave them more time to do it. It gave them a freer rein about the house, and he told Dorinda to bathe them.

She didn't understand what he was up to. He tortured the new children relentlessly and only cast the painful spell upon those in her cage once every three or four days. But she wasn't complaining.

With her no longer being forced to clean only the library and foyer it allowed her to explore. The first day of her expanded freedoms she looked into not only all the manor's sleeping quarters, but Master Ruddick's rooms as well.

The immensity of the Master's bedroom intimidated her. His four-post, black wood bed was so large she had difficulty making it as Dorinda showed her. She thought all the children could sprawl on it and not even come close to touching. Several brass lamps hung from all four red paneled walls, a multitude of small tables lining them. All the furniture appeared to be cut from the same dark-red wood as did the door trim. And most stunning, the ceiling was painted to look like a lovely blue sky with a smattering of multicolored clouds.

After making the bed—she had to climb atop it to do the job—she tied open the thick curtains covering a large window that overlooked the stable yard. A light snow fell outside, covering everything in a thin layer of white. It was a view of the grounds she'd never witnessed before. She saw Kos mucking out a fenced-in area filled with pigs on one side of the stables, and on the other lay a small building with chickens coming in and out of it.

On the opposite wall from the window, a twisted looking door opened into what Dorinda said was the Master's own private chapel to the Lord of Chaos. The odd room's interior was of no particular shape, having many oddly angled walls that appeared to be made of black stone with a dull sheen. Nooks and crevices covered the walls, catching and reflecting some of the light of the thirteen torches scattered about the room. Others areas were filled with nothing but darkness.

At the center of the chapel stood a black, fluted pedestal. Atop the pedestal, within a thick nest of thin metal rods, sat a globe about double the size of an adult's fist. The globe appeared to be made of glass and she saw wisps of multi-colored light flowing within it.

As she walked about the room, she couldn't help but to go look at the glass ball. The tiny wisps of light were mesmerizing. She walked around it, trying to inspect it from every direction. And with each step she moved closer and closer to it. It seemed to beckon to her.

"Come to me," a feather soft whisper echoed in her mind. "Forsake the Mother and be mine."

As she reached out, the dancing light pulling her ever forward, she felt a light current of air caress the back of her head. The voice evaporated from her mind. She turned toward the door and saw nothing, but she felt as though eyes were upon her. From every dark nook and cranny where the light failed to pierce she felt something sinister leering at her and laughing. She saw nothing. She heard nothing. Yet she felt it. She bolted for the door, not even bothering to close it behind her.

The following day she told Nash that she wasn't going into the Master's room again. When the boy asked her why she said, "I just don't like it. That weird room off his bedroom… there's just something wrong with it."

"What do you mean?" Nash asked. "I think the Master's rooms are great. Did you even look out that window? It's like you can see forever."

"I'm not talking about his bedroom, I'm talking about that holy room. The entire time in there made my skin crawl. And I swear to you I was being watched, but there wasn't anyone there." The Girl still felt unclean from stepping into that room.

"What are you talking about? It was probably just Acey nosing about," Nash said.

"No," she urged. "I'm telling you there was no one there. But I still felt something looking at me."

"I've been in there lots of times and I have no idea what you're talking about," Nash replied, doubt filling his voice.

"If you like it so much then you clean it," she told him in a huff and stormed off.

That second day the Girl discovered a room she truly found odd on the outermost wall of the manor, near to Master Ruddick's chambers. The dark interior smelled quite foul, and flies buzzed near a hole cut in the top of a short wooden bench sitting along one wall. Along the other wall sat a table with a wash basin next to a cake of soap and two cloths.

When she asked Dorinda what the room was for, the Girl could scarcely believe it. "He poops in there?" she said, taken aback. "He doesn't use a pot?"

"Of course he does, don't be silly, but he only uses one during the night," the cook replied. "That room is where you'll take Master Ruddick's chamber pot and dump it into the hole. It's called a privy, and it's only for the Master and his guests."

Sometimes Master Ruddick had guests come to the manor, but it wasn't often. They came by coach or by horseback and asked for him at the door. She, or one of the other children, would run and tell Dorinda who then informed the Master.

Most often these guests simply stopped by and asked after his health or if he had discovered anything new. The Girl did her best not to listen in on the conversations because the Master would strike out at them for dawdling. Truthfully, she avoided it mostly because what they talked about made her feel uneasy for some reason. On occasion, these guests stayed and spent the night. Sometimes the visitor would be a young woman who Master Ruddick would usher upstairs where they spent the rest of the day and night.

One particular day a man came riding in hard. Before Kos took the man's horse he jumped down and ran into the manor, not even bothering to ring the bell.

"Where is Ruddick? I must see him at once," he said to her after flinging open the door. "Go fetch him and be quick about it. There's a Chaos Storm on its way!"

The Girl's blood ran cold, and she dashed for the basement. Several children had spoken about seeing a Chaos Storm. They said the storms were acts of the Lord, the place where the Great Lord of Chaos reached out and physically touched the world.

Her bare feet slapped on the stairs as she ran, nearly falling in her haste. She sprinted to the back of the basement, a place she thankfully never saw before, and ran to Master Ruddick as he bent over a bloodstained table. On the table sat a hare in a small cage.

"Master Ruddick," she called, huffing as she ran up and pulled on his dark-gray robes.

"What the hells are you doing back here?" he screamed. "Get back to your work before I do something to you I'll later regret!"

"A man has arrived," she said, shaking. "He said a Chaos Storm is on the way!"

Master Ruddick's eyes grew wide. "Quickly, run and tell Dorinda to get you all into your cage," he said as he raced for the stairs. The fear and excitement in the Master's eyes was evident. But his excitement alarmed the Girl far more than his fear.

The Girl sprinted up the stairs, the Master outdistancing her, and ran to Dorinda. She told the cook of the storm and their Master's command.

"Oh sweet Lord," she said. "Where are the others?"

"Nash and Dak are upstairs, and I think Acey's in the library," she replied hastily.

"You go get Acey. I'll get the others. Go quickly, we haven't much time!"

The Girl raced down the hallways and into the vast library where she found Acey standing stock-still, staring out the window. She sprinted up to Acey and grabbed her about the shoulders. "We have to get to the basement, quickly!"

Acey pointed out the window, her voice a mixture of awe and fear. "What is it?"

She pulled Acey away from the window. "There's no time! Go," she shouted, and gave her a shove toward the door. The Girl knew she should follow suit, but she found she couldn't resist the urge to look out the window herself. What she saw terrified her.

The sky roiled with a tumultuous tableau of boiling black, gray, and red clouds. The wailing wind pierced her ears. It sounded as if the air itself were screaming in agony.

Jagged strokes of lightning stabbed into the woods near the manor, setting fires in over a dozen places. A bolt struck a short way down the road. It cracked the ground and turned it molten, shining in a multitude of colors.

She saw a slender funnel extending out of the clouds, like a gnarled black and red finger. It tore into the trees and everything it touched became deformed. It turned the trees a blackish-brown and twisted them into knots. The animals it touched became mutated into hideous creatures only the Lord of Chaos delighted in seeing.

The Girl tried to go, to flee for her life, but her feet seemed frozen to the floor in terror. Her body shook and her heart raced; it tried to beat itself out of her chest. Her breath heaved raggedly and her mind blanked. She knew she would not live to see the next few minutes.

Master Ruddick burst out the front door of the manor and ran toward the horrific oncoming storm. She thought he'd gone mad. He stopped and raised his hands into the air, out of which floated a ball of glass. She recognized it as the globe from his chapel. It hovered above his head for only a moment before shooting up into the hellish maelstrom.

When the globe reached the center of those clouds a loud clap shattered the cacophony as though the sky cracked open. The clouds swirled, moving faster and faster, spinning into a great, thin disk of black, gray, and red. The disk then shrunk in on itself before flashing out of existence.

She saw the globe fall from the sky and hit the ground with a dull thud. Master Ruddick ran to it and levitated it until it hung before his face. Master Ruddick's globe was changed. Its inner light had changed to a bright swirling torrent of color and shade. It seemed as though the entire Chaos Storm now lay within the globe.

Master Ruddick's eyes blazed triumphantly. Deep down she knew all their lives were about to change.

In the days following the storm, Master Ruddick acquired more and more children for his experiments. In three weeks he went through fifteen new children—fifteen more corpses to be thrown upon the pile. He needed to enlist Kos's aid in carrying away the bodies from the basement. The Girl and her three cellmates couldn't keep up the maintenance of the house while at the same time deal with the cleaning required with the refuse in the basement laboratory.

Acey spoke up one night, as the Girl lay under her skins trying to sleep, "I don't know how much longer I can take this," she said in her high, melodious voice. "Their screaming night and day. I just can't take it anymore."

The Girl sat up and looked at Acey. The light from the few rough torches Master Ruddick kept lit at night cast dark shadows on Acey's face as she sat with her back against the bars. "What choice do we have?" the Girl asked her drowsily.

"I don't know," Acey replied. "It's like I can feel their pain. Every time they scream I remember how it feels to me and it hurts all over again."

The Girl sympathized with her. She felt the same way. "I know, just go to sleep."

Acey then added disquietly, "His tortures don't seem to hurt as much anymore." She looked at the Girl. "What do you think it means?"

The Girl didn't know, but hearing it from Acey struck her. She too felt the spells were not as painful as they once were. She thought it was just her imagination. She figured hearing the others constant screams somehow made her numb to it all. But if Acey felt the same thing…

"How long has it felt that way?" the Girl asked Acey.

"For weeks now," she answered with a sigh. "Why?"

"Because I noticed it just the other day," the Girl replied numbly.

"What do you think it means?" Acey pleaded.

"I don't know," the Girl said softly, shaking her head. "We should get to sleep."

"Can I ask you something?" Acey asked as she lay back down. "What's wrong with Nash?"

The Girl didn't know that either. He hadn't spoken in days and went about his chores woodenly. "Just go to sleep," the Girl murmured, trying her best to sound reassuring, but it sounded hollow in her ears. She pulled her furs about her tight, trying to close out the world.

She took some time to fall asleep and her dreams were disturbed. All about her demons and ghosts screamed, filling her world. And she saw nothing but swirling colors and the faces of the howling children. Whenever she tried to run, she felt herself being pulled back, then pulled forward, and then from below and above. The voices and colors seeped into her and she felt it tearing her apart. The Girl didn't know where she was, she only knew she needed to get out.

She started awake with a clanging on the bars of their cage. "Time to get up," Master Ruddick declared. He didn't sound happy. "Time to get your asses to work."

The Girl stood with a groan. She rarely remembered her dreams but that one still clung to her. She waited behind Nash as the Master opened the door. The boy took only a single step out of the cage before Master Ruddick grasped him by the face.

"What's this?" the Master asked with a smile, his voice filling with excitement. "Well, it seems I finally have my answer." He pulled Nash to the side and pointed at the rest. "You three go about your work."

As they climbed the stairs the Girl asked fearfully, "Why is he taking Nash?"

"His eyes had changed color," Dak answered, his voice stilted.

The Girl nearly missed a step and stumbled. It was the same thing that had happened to Rosh. First, he become withdrawn, then his eyes started changing color. Whatever Master Ruddick was doing, it was changing them.

For days they walked on eggshells, or so it felt. They saw nothing of either Nash or Master Ruddick, and the entire time no noise came from the back of that basement. No sounds from the animals, no screams, nothing.

Dorinda let them out of their cages in the mornings and put them in at night. She became quite a sweet woman. For a long time Dorinda used to be very distant. However, ever since they got preferential treatment the cook warmed, yet at the same time, she grew sadder as well.

"What's wrong?" the Girl asked the cook one day.

"Nothing, child," she said as she made her way around the kitchen. "You three just finish up eating and then head on back down."

She allowed them to take all their meals at the table in the kitchen rather than eating them below.

The Girl finished her last bite of sharp cheese, washed it down with the ewe's milk, and headed back down the stairs, quickly followed by the rest. She ducked into the cage and rolled up in her corner. When she woke the next morning she did her best to not cry when she saw Nash's body upon the pile.

.

Chapter 3

Rekindling

With her brother's death and their recent newfound freedoms about the manor, the Girl found she was feeling for her cellmates. She realized that, like herself, they were lonely and frightened. She could actually sense how they felt. The Girl knew Acey dearly missed her family who she said had died in some kind of war betwixt two city-states. And she felt Dak's profound loneliness and utter isolation having been there so long.

But with Nash's death the Girl drew in on herself once more. She pushed Acey away, refusing to answer her questions and reassure her. The Girl knew she was breaking Acey's heart, but she didn't care. She couldn't afford to.

Besides, the Girl felt Acey's soul was going to be crushed eventually anyway, so the sooner it happened the better.

She didn't have to push Dak away. He was starting to resemble Nash before his eyes turned color. He wouldn't talk unless he absolutely had to, and he plodded about his work. She knew it was only a matter of time for him.

Over the following weeks, Ruddick brought in more and more children to experiment on. In those weeks the Girl was surprised to see one of them actually survived. And much to her sorrow the Master placed him in their cage.

The first night the boy cried till dawn before passing out. When the boy wouldn't wake up in the morning as Dorinda came for them, the Girl figured he had died. Yet when Dorinda asked Master Ruddick what she should do, he said the boy was too exhausted to awaken.

"Just leave him be for now," Ruddick instructed in a surprisingly moderate tone. "He'll join them tomorrow. In the meantime get the others fed and off to work. I've much to do."

When the Girl returned for the evening she saw the Master was right. The boy sat in the cage, wide awake. "I'm Samuel," he said, making his introductions. "But my friends just call me Sam." His voice began sweet and melodious then changed. His expression darkened. "At least they used to. Jonny and Tessa died the first night here." His face then lit back up. "But you all can be my new friends!"

The Girl wanted nothing to do with him. She cringed when he gave his name along with those of his dead friends. She didn't want to know the names of children on the pile of dead, she knew too many as it was.

The Girl didn't like how his chatty, gregarious nature made her want to smile. Nor did she like that for a brief moment she found the boy's dark eyes and hair quite pretty. She smothered the thought, ruthlessly. She didn't care if the boy was cute. Eventually, he was going to be dead like everyone else.

So she turned her back on him, crawled into her corner and pulled her furs about her, trying her best to go to sleep. But it wasn't easy. She couldn't shut out their voices.

"I'm Acey and that's Dak," Acey said before adding quietly, "but Dak doesn't really talk anymore."

"What's her name?" the boy asked.

"I don't know," Acey replied somewhat hurt. "I don't think she has one. If she does she never said it."

The Girl heard the spark of desperation in Acey's voice. Acey wanted someone to interact with her, someone to bond with. It sent a pang of guilt into the Girl's stomach until she stomped on it. It was better to feel nothing, she tried to convince herself.

"Why don't you have a name?" the boy asked, but she refused to answer.

"Her parents never gave her one," Acey stated with a bit of a sneer.

"How long have you been here?" the boy asked.

"I don't know," Acey said. "After a while you lose count."

"How long have you been here?" he asked the Girl.

But she just curled up tighter and ignored him.

"Is she all right?" the boy asked, the concern plain in his voice.

"She's just being mean," Acey said. "She thinks she's better than me and doesn't want to talk to me anymore. She's not like Dak. There's something wrong with him. He's become just like Nash did before the Master took him away."

When Sam inquired about Nash, Acey told him the entire story while the Girl fought off the tears. In the end, the Girl had grown to like Nash. He found humor in almost anything. As she listened to Acey talk about his death, it was like living it all over again.

That feeling was driven home even harder the next morning when they found Dak did not wake up. He had died in his sleep.

As the week progressed, the boy—she refused to think of him by name—constantly tried to talk to her. Whenever he came near her he asked how she was or where did she came from. He asked her what her favorite color was and about her dreams. He even wanted to know about her favorite food. Whoever heard of such a thing? It drove her crazy.

And every time he tried to engage her, he gently touched her on the hand, arm, or shoulder. It made her cringe.

The first time he touched her she pulled back as though burned and stared daggers at him. Yet it only seemed to encourage the boy. Several times a day he walked up to her and talked as though they were having a conversation. However, she refused to say a word. He talked, and she ignored him.

After a time though she realized she stopped pulling away from his touch. And to her own horror, she found she looked forward to it, and his presence.

The worst part, in her estimation, was the boy's interactions seemed to encourage Acey, who copied Sam—the boy—in everything he did, and started talking to her again.

She even went a step further. At night Acey sat next to the Girl as they lay down to sleep. Acey hummed to her while stroking her hair. She said it was something her mother used to do. Deep down, even though the Girl tried to harden herself, she truly loved Acey for doing it.

Acey and the boy grew so tight they even held hands whenever possible. They tickled one another and chased each other about the house when they had time. At night they lay together, wrapped in each other's arms beneath the furs. And once she even saw him give her a kiss, making Acey giggle and blush.

Once the two became inseparable they ganged up on her. Not in any cruel way. They did everything they could to engage her. And the harder she pushed them away the harder they tried to draw her out.

They would both talk to her and gently touch her in the process. And at night they slept with her. She stayed wrapped tightly in her furs, trying to push them away, but they lay upon either side of her; Acey wedged herself between the Girl and the cage bars while the boy lay against her back. They wrapped their arms about her and held her close as Acey hummed. The Girl fell asleep in a cocoon of their warm embrace.

One night, surrounded by warmth and affection, she realized all the contact and affection was more than she could take. Her walls crumbled, and she gave in.

"Thank you," she murmured, her voice cracking and her eyes damp with tears. "Thank you, Acey," she gave her a kiss on the cheek, "and, Sam," she said as he pulled his arms about her tighter. She slept soundly that night, her dreams pleasant and warm.

When she woke the next morning she realized something rather astonishing. She had been so preoccupied with her trying to hold everyone away that she hadn't noticed Master Ruddick was no longer acquiring more children. She also realized that after Samuel had joined them, the Master no longer performed his experiments on them.

The thought scared her at first. She was sure Master Ruddick would redouble his efforts on them once he had run out of his new children. But it wasn't the case. He merely came down to the basement from time to time and do things with some of the animals a couple of times a week. But nothing more. He spent most of his time in his rooms, either alone or with the occasional woman visitor.

"Sam?" the Girl asked one night as they all lay together beneath their pile of furs. "Why do you think Master Ruddick stopped?"

Sam gave a shrug. "I don't know. Maybe he got bored. Maybe he found what he was looking for."

She tried to accept Sam's explanation but couldn't. She felt Acey did, but for some reason the Girl couldn't. She also held a sinking feeling Sam didn't believe it either.

"So is it true that you don't have a name?" Sam asked.

The Girl shrunk in on herself a little. "Yes," she said softly. "I guess they didn't think I was worth naming."

"What happened to them?"

"I don't know. I don't even remember them."

"Really?"

"Yes, really," she snapped. "I don't remember them and I don't want to. I just hope they're dead. I hope they died screaming. It's what they deserve for doing this to me."

"I'm sorry," Sam said. He hugged her tightly until she drifted off to sleep.

A month passed and nothing changed. They went about their daily chores. Dorinda smiled once more. She gazed upon the children with hope in her eyes. Much to the Girl's delight, she didn't have to put up with Kos's leers as he no longer had a reason to come into the manor. And even on the rare occasion when she saw him out in the stable yard, the stableman quickly looked away. She figured Dorinda had finally put him in his place.

One day the Girl stood in the foyer polishing the table below the Master's large mirror. She was bending down, rubbing oils in its legs, when Sam startled her.

"So, just how long do you think you've been here?" he asked. His voice sounded inquisitive yet intense and serious.

The Girl jerked upright, banging her head on the underside of the table in the process. She gave out a curse, the worst she knew, and grasped her head. Clenching her teeth tightly she kept her eyes closed until the pain faded some. She expected Sam to comfort her, but he simply stood there, peering at her.

"What?" she asked sharply.

"I said, how long do you think you've been here?" His voice was light but measured.

"Six years, I think," she replied as she rubbed her head.

"That would make you around ten, then." His lips held a small smile, like he had some big secret and refused to share it with her.

"Yeah, so?"

"Don't be angry," he said. His chin dropped to his chest, and a quiver grew in his voice. "I was just curious, that's all. Acey doesn't seem to remember much, so I thought I'd ask you." His voice quivered, and he appeared to be on the edge of tears, yet she had her doubts. Sam cried. Tears flowed down his cheeks, and he ran the back of his hand across his sniffling nose.

And yet still, deep down, she felt it was fake. She just knew. "Why are you doing this? I don't want to play."

Samuel's crying stopped. In a flash his face was normal, his tears gone, as though he hadn't been crying at all. His eyes beamed with excitement and he held a hooded smile. "You know it's not real, don't you? You should have been trying to comfort me as you would have with Acey. But you're not." He cocked his head to the side. "Why?"

"Because I could see you were playing with me," she replied. How dare the little turd try and mess with her like that!

"No, you couldn't," Sam said smoothly. "There was no way for you to see through the illusion, it was too perfect." His smile then became broad. "You can feel it, can't you? You can sense how I'm feeling right this moment. Yes, I can see it in your eyes." His face was positively beaming. "Your wonderfully Chaos blessed eyes."

The Girl stared at him in confusion. Her head throbbed, and her legs grew weak as she watched Samuel walk away. Her jaw went slack as he dissolved, his form twisting and stretching, growing larger.

Halfway across the room, Samuel turned and laughed, deep and rich. Samuel, no longer a child, gazed at her with ice-blue eyes. His dead black robes nearly matched his coal dark skin. His full head of hair was now nothing but bare scalp.

"Yes," the man said, his voice deep and slick, "Ruddick will want to know just how well he has succeeded with you." He cocked his head and tried to sound reassuring,

"Don't be sad, child. You should be happy. The Great Lord has blessed you. It's in your eyes." He laughed again and walked up the stairs of the manor.

The Girl had no idea what was going on. "My eyes?" she muttered as she turned and looked at herself in the mirror. Horror ripped through her as her eyes slowly changed color, from brown to blue to gray.

The room spun, and she hit the floor with a thud. The world went black.

Sorrow's Heart   G. S. Scott

Chapter 4

The Lord's Blessing

The Girl stood at Dorinda's side as Master Ruddick spoke to the black-robed priest at the front door. "Thank you again for your aid in my experiment."

"It was my pleasure, rest assured," Samuel replied oily, his face split with a wicked smile. "And I wish to thank you for my recompense."

The Girl fought back tears, heartbroken, as she watched the priest stroke Acey's hair who stood quivering beside him. Dorinda told her that Acey now belonged to the priest in black. The cook told her she'd seen the priest before, quite some time ago. They'd trained together as acolytes at a place called Gate Keep, far to the north.

The Girl would miss Acey's humming to her as she slept.

"You will tell me if she also exhibits any wonderful manifestations of the Great Lord, won't you?" Master Ruddick asked.

"Absolutely," Samuel replied. "I believe that your manipulations have already changed this, oh so lovely girl." He ran a finger across Acey's cheek. "And we shall know soon to what end. I will continue gently as you have shown me and we shall see what comes of it."

"Just remember to be careful," Master Ruddick cautioned. "You were never as skilled as I in this area. You don't want to do any permanent harm to her."

"Oh, believe me, Rudy, I will be extra careful." He glanced down at Acey, cupped her chin, and made her look up at him. "I want to share a lifetime of pleasures with this perfect child." He ran his thumb across Acey's lower lip before returning his gaze to Master Ruddick's and nodded. "Until I see you again."

The Girl watched them both climb aboard the priest's carriage. As the door shut, the driver flicked the horse's reins, and they headed down the road. She doubted she would ever see her friend again. She was now truly alone.

Master Ruddick then turned and spoke to Dorinda. "Go to town tomorrow and get her several dresses, both formal and for housework." He pulled a sealed piece of parchment from his robes and handed it to her. "Give this to the dressmaker. It's a list of what I'm looking for regarding the formalwear. I leave the rest up to you. I also want you to bathe her regularly, and for her to clean her teeth. I want her to be presentable at all times."

"Yes, Master Ruddick," the cook said with a bow. "Will we be acquiring any more children now that she is alone?"

Master Ruddick paused a moment. "No, not at this time. I didn't want to part with her but Samuel was insistent. However, while you're there, let it be known we're looking for help."

He then glanced down at the Girl. "I know you thought our little ruse to be cruel, but I had to know for certain. You children certainly weren't about to tell me on your own. I'm no fool."

He knelt down to look at her eye to eye. "I want you to understand this," he said, placing a hand upon her shoulder. "You are proof that my experiments work, that the Lord's blessing can be passed to a mundane. You are now my most prized possession and will be well cared for. You have become empathic, as well, and I wish to see if I can expand upon that. It will be difficult and painful but you will persevere. You have strength."

Smiling, he stood once more and added as though to himself, "Fascinating how the boys changed first yet it was the girls whose minds survived." He walked up the stairs.

The Girl had no idea what he was talking about other than the pain. She knew that all too well. And if he thought her so special why did he always torture her so? He knew she would 'persevere'? She didn't know what that meant. She only wished she had one of the cook's knives so she could stab him in the face!

She stood there and stared at the door until Dorinda placed her hand gently on her shoulder. "Come along," she said with a smile. "Let's get you washed up and then to your room. You'll find it infinitely better than your old cage."

Freshly scrubbed, she padded behind Dorinda to her new room. It was one of the secondary bedrooms in the upper halls, and she had it all to herself. It had a large four post bed that sat along the wall opposite a large hearth. The dark paneled walls contrasted sharply with the sky-blue ceiling, and thick, bright red curtains that covered the window which overlooked the front of the manor.

After placing the lamp she carried on the bedside table, the cook helped the Girl into the high bed and tucked her in. "Sleep well now, little one," the cook whispered as she gently ran her hand through the Girl's hair with a smile. She then turned down the lamp and left.

The Girl didn't like the room's mammoth size. It made her feel far too exposed on the too soft and lumpy bed. So she pulled all the sheets and blankets off the bed and curled up against the wall next to the hearth. She found the popping and snapping of the fire strangely soothing.

After feeding her, Dorinda left her alone for the first time to head into town. The Girl went about her work in the manor but she felt pressed for time now having to do it all herself. When the cook returned soon after midday, the Girl was working in the foyer. Dorinda's face beamed with joy. She carried a pair of burlap bags and several boxes.

"Come along," she said to the Girl as she headed for the stairs to the second floor. Once in the Girl's new room, Dorinda huffed at seeing the bedding on the floor. "After we put you into one of these dresses, we will put the others away in the wardrobe. Then, you will remake that bed. What were you thinking?"

When the Girl told her about how it made her feel, Dorinda sighed. "This is a big change for you, I know. But believe me, in time you will find the bed far better than sleeping on the floor." She then smiled and gently caressed the Girl's hair.

After a time the Girl got used to sleeping on the bed, but she had difficulty finding the softness comfortable. The pillow took her some time getting used to, as well. But mostly she just couldn't get over the feeling that the room was far too large. She huddled completely under the covers to get away from the agoraphobic feeling.

She took a while to get used to wearing dresses as well. The ones that fell to her knees weren't bad, aside from the constant tugging to just get it to feel right, but the ones that hung down to her feet she couldn't stand. She continuously tripped in them, particularly when she needed to run.

She rather liked wearing slippers. Her feet didn't hurt as much at the end of the day and they kept her warm. Plus, she liked the whisking sound they made as she crossed a room. She hated the stockings Dorinda gave her and steadfastly refused to wear them. And since Master Ruddick didn't seem to care one way or the other on the subject, she gladly went without.

A month had passed since she lost Acey, and other than her surroundings and clothing, her life remained unchanged. She still worked most days cleaning the manor, though she took two to three times longer to do all the work herself, and she continued to endure the Master's experiments. She still wasn't allowed outside the manor, and Kos's disgusting stares continued to bother her.

One early morning as the Girl scrubbed the foyer floor on her hands and knees, Master Ruddick came down the central stairs with his globe, the one he'd cast into the Chaos storm, hovering above his right hand. Lights of all colors and shades danced and swirled within the globe's glassy interior. It made her shiver.

"Come with me," he said nonchalantly. "We've work to do."

She promptly stood and followed him through the manor and into the basement. She hated these sessions but at least he only did then twice a week or so. The man may have looked and sounded casual, but she felt excitement bubbling inside him and it made her worry.

He took to the basement and placed her on the stool next to the table where he did his most extensive experiments upon. She hated the deep brown table, stained black with the blood of the many animals that died on it. As well as the blood of Nash and Rosh, she had no doubt.

Once seated, he placed the cage of his prize black hare upon the table. It surprised her. Most of the animals he slaughtered with a whim, but a few, like that hare, he treated with extra care. Not unlike how he had been treating her as of late, she realized. Between her and the caged hare he placed his globe on a metal nest just like the one in his room.

The Master concentrated upon the globe and the thing glowed stronger. He lazily waved his hands in front of the globe before moving them toward her. Her head instantly hurt, a pulsing throb behind her eyes and she gritted her teeth so as not to make a sound.

When Ruddick waved his left hand toward the hare, she threw her head back and screamed. The throb became a piercing pain in her mind. She felt millions of white hot needles stabbing into her head and swirl about the inside of her skull. It felt like she was being ripped out of her own body. She thrashed about and fell to the floor. Her entire world consisted of only pain.

Two days later she sat on her stool in front of the mirror in her room, still feeling weak. Dorinda stood behind her, calmly brushing her hair. She had blacked out from the pain and the Master left her down in the basement that first night. Dorinda told her the Master had Kos set up a cot next to the fire for the night before carrying her up to her room the next morning. She remembered none of it.

She stared at her eyes in the mirror as they slowly changed from color to color at random. She hated them, her cursed eyes. The Lord of Chaos had danced about her so much he changed her into one of his own. And even though she felt the emotions of most anyone she looked at, she still felt alone.

She felt no connection to anyone in that manor, not even Dorinda. No matter how much the cook doted on her, the Girl felt almost nothing for the woman. Dorinda was trying to be a mother to her, and she didn't like it. The Girl hated her mother, so no matter how hard Dorinda tried it would make little difference to the Girl. Still, she tried her best to appease the cook. Just because she didn't feel for the woman didn't mean she couldn't at least try and be nice.

As the Girl sat there, she felt Dorinda's disappointment. She apparently wasn't very convincing at playing nice. She also felt the woman's concern, and it made the Girl glance down in shame. Dorinda wanted nothing from her and cared about her wellbeing. Yet the Girl was still unwilling to return even the tiniest amount of feeling. She had none to give.

"How are you feeling today, my dear?" Dorinda asked.

"Better," she replied weakly.

"Well, Master Ruddick said he wants you to remain in bed until at least tomorrow." Dorinda then looked down, and the Girl felt the concern rise sharply. "He said he will come check on you in the morning."

She set the brush down on the side table and helped the Girl to her feet. "Let's get you into bed and then I'll build up the fire a little bigger. It's turning a bit cold as of late and I don't want you succumbing to it."

After Dorinda closed the door behind her, the Girl slid down to the center of the bed, pulling the multiple layers of covers up over her head. It felt natural, like being huddled in her own burrow.

That night she dreamt of tunnels and burrows, and the comfort of snuggling down into a bed of shed fur. She ran about the tall grass, playing with her brothers and sisters, all the while keeping ever vigilant with her long ears. Her constantly twitching nose kept testing for scents in the air.

Shock and fear struck her as the sky turned red and the world spun all about. Her head strummed with pain, a pulsing throb like the beat of a heart. The ground shook beneath her four furry feet—

Her eyes snapped open and gazed upon a roughhewn ceiling. She was no longer buried under her covers in her room. Instead she lay in a small bed next to the basement hearth. Master Ruddick sat a short distance away at his bench, his hand atop the black hare's cage and his eyes closed tight.

Her pain vanished the moment she opened her eyes. "How did I get here?" she asked, bewildered.

"I carried you," Master Ruddick said softly as he opened his eyes, a wide smile playing upon his face. "You were dreaming, and I sensed a residual energy flowing out of you. So I brought you down here. You were sleeping quite soundly," he finished with a laugh. His high level of excitement frightened the Girl.

"D-do you want me to sit on my stool, Master?" she asked.

"No, my child. That will not be necessary. I was merely reading the flows between you and the hare." He cocked his head to the side. "What did you dream about?"

She relaxed, relieved she would not have to undergo such a painful experience so soon. She told him of her simple dream, adding, "I think I was a rabbit?"

The Master's excitement spiked. "Excellent! That's because you were, my dear. The energy I felt flowing out of you led me to my little friend here. There is now a connection between you and the hare."

She stared at Master Ruddick in disbelief.

A thought blossomed into her mind. "I do believe this charlatan has gone mad."

Her eyes widened in shock. That thought had not been hers. She gaped at the hare who stared back at her in equal disbelief.

Sorrow's Heart — G. S. Scott

Chapter 5

Jasper

The Girl could scarcely believe it. She stared at the hare. It must have been her imagination. Perhaps she was still dreaming? There was simply no way she could have heard the hare's thoughts.

"Can you actually hear me, little girl?" the voice once again entered her mind. "By the Mother, I believe you can?"

The Girl shook her head violently. She didn't want to believe it. Was she losing her mind?

"What is it?" the Master asked. "I can see something happening. What are you experiencing?"

The Girl didn't want to answer. She couldn't. If she answered then she would be admitting to herself it was real. "Nothing, Master," she squeaked.

"Don't give me that," he roared. "I can see the flow between you two. I can read your face. What is happening?"

She just closed her eyes and shook her head.

The Master's eyes raged. He lifted his hand then looked at it uncertainly. His eyes flicked back to the Girl then slapped her hard across the face. "Tell me."

She didn't answer. Her left ear rang and her cheek burned from the blow, but she said nothing.

Shaking his hand in pain, the Master looked about the room. His eyes went to the blood-soaked table. He quickly ran a finger along the very edge of the table, smoke trailing it from one end to the other. A thin piece fell to the floor. He bent over and picked it up. "You will answer me!" He jerked her off her seat with his other hand.

The Girl worked her mouth, but no sounds came out. None of this was real. It just couldn't be.

"Stop that. She's just a child," the voice echoed into her mind.

The Girl closed her eyes and shook her head again.

Sharp pain exploded from her behind as the Master struck her with the makeshift switch. She screamed out in pain.

"Tell me, damn you. I can see it as clear as day. Tell me what's happening." He struck her time and again across her rear.

The Girl could take no more. "He talked to me," she cried out. "I heard him talk to me!" The Girl then crumpled to the floor as the Master released her from his grip. She curled up into a ball, not wanting to believe any of it. What did it mean? What did he do to her?

"It's all right, little one," the hare said to her in soothing tones. "He's stopped. I don't know what he did but you'll be all right."

"I did it," the Master exclaimed. "I knew it would work." He stood over her as she lay on the cold, stone floor. "The next time I ask you something you will answer me. Do you understand? This is far too important for you to be holding out on me." He bent over and gently helped her to her feet. "Go lie on your bed near the fire. I'll have the cook bring you something for the welts. I can't afford anything happening to you." He escorted her to her bed and left, smiling.

She curled up into a ball upon the bed, shivering in pain and anger. She wiped the tears from her eyes. Never before had the Master punished her physically, and she didn't understand why. Why didn't he just use his powers?

"He probably didn't want to risk jeopardizing his work," the hare said to her. "If he struck at you with Chaos, there might have been adverse effects. Not to mention he might have killed you."

She refused to acknowledge him. Instead, she stared into the flames.

"What's your name, little one?" he asked. "I am Jasper."

She curled up tighter and refused to answer.

After a short time, Dorinda came down into the basement. She stripped the Girl of her dress and applied some kind of ointment to the welts on her bottom and the backs of her legs. Once finished she gave her a slightly bitter drink, then gently laid her hand upon the Girl's head. "Now you get some sleep. When you feel up to it, you can go to your room."

The Girl quickly slipped into unconsciousness. Her dreams started out dark and disturbed but quickly changed to ones of tranquility. In one she simply dreamt of a tree; a massive, beautiful, and all-encompassing tree.

For several days afterward, the Girl lazed in a minor state of shock. Even after telling the Master the truth, it took quite some time to admit the truth to herself. She didn't want to believe it. It was one thing to find out she read peoples' emotions, but quite another to find out he had turned her into some kind of freak.

In the following weeks Maser Ruddick expanded his experiments on her. He used all of his other animals, occasionally even using multiple ones at a time. With most of them she merely found the experience painful, something she'd almost grown accustomed to, but whenever he used the hare, the pain was crippling.

A day following a particularly rough experience with the hare, Master Ruddick sat on her bed, gently caressing her hair. "I'm sorry for our last treatment. It was far more difficult on you than I had anticipated." He then stroked her shoulder, a small smile playing on his face. "The last thing I want is for anything untoward happening to you."

Untoward? His odd attention made her feel very uncomfortable. He'd not acted that way with her in the past. And there was a gleam in his eye she found terrifying.

"Yet I'm afraid that they must continue." He tucked the sheets up about her shoulders. "It would appear that our working with the others animals is gaining us little. But working with the hare, no matter how uncomfortable—"

"Jasper," she interrupted him. The word popped out of her mouth before she even realized it.

Master Ruddick seemed taken aback. He appeared angry at first for being interrupted, but he cocked his head slightly and asked, "Why would you give the hare a name? And why that one of all things?"

"I didn't give it to him. That's what he told me it was."

"The hare said its name is Jasper? Fascinating." He looked at her a moment then stood. "Get some rest, my precious. We shall speak again later."

She woke when a young, tanned skinned man with dark hair, wearing nondescript gray breeches and shirt walked into her room with a cage in his hands.

"Hello, young miss." He placed the cage upon the bedside table. "My name is Kenneth. I am the Master's new houseboy and will be taking over your work," he finished with a bow. He appeared several years older than her but was not yet a full grown man.

Her mind, still fuzzy from the previous day's session, left the Girl confused. She glanced at the cage the young man brought and became even more confused when she saw it held Jasper. "What's going on?" she asked somewhat fearfully.

If the Master wanted Jasper brought in to her room, it meant he planned to move the sessions up there. And as she often soiled herself during sessions with Jasper, it meant she would need to do even more cleaning there than usual.

When she soiled herself in the basement, they simply threw sawdust and dirt over the mess and swept it away. That would not be as easy to do on the Master's nice wood floors in her room.

"The Master bid me bring you your pet and tell you that I will be taking over most of your duties, Mistress," he said with another bow.

Mistress? she thought. She became even more confused. Pushing her sheets off, she climbed out of bed, and her legs gave way as her head spun. The young man grabbed her to keep her from falling to the floor. Once she regained her balance she frowned. He stared at her the way Kos often did and she sensed an excitement in his mind. She hastily pulled on the dress lying at the foot of her bed.

Over the past few months her body changed along with her mind. Her chest had grown, and she sprouted hair between her legs. And the young man's leer made her uncomfortable about the changes. She was becoming a freak. She felt his desires as easily as she heard Jasper's thoughts. She felt for certain it meant she was turning into an animal.

"Don't be silly," Jasper said in her mind.

"I'm not being silly," she yelled at the cage.

The young man looked at her queerly. "I'm sorry, Mistress. I did not mean to cause you any distress. I do not think you silly at all."

"I wasn't talking to you," she snapped

"You are being silly," Jasper interjected. "You are not turning into one of that insane priest's unfortunate subjects in the basement."

"I'm sorry, Mistress, but I don't understand," the young man said with a shake of his head at the same time Jasper spoke into her mind.

"What? No, stop! I can only hear you one at a time," she shouted, and rocked her head, immediately regretting it as pain blossomed into her mind. She grabbed the bed to keep from falling. When the young man walked to her to help support her she pushed him away. "Don't!"

"Yes, Mistress," he said again with a nod of the head.

"What's your name?" the Girl asked once more as the pain subsided.

"Again, I am Kenneth, Mistress."

"Why do you keep calling me that?"

"I am sorry," he replied smoothly. "What title would you like me to call you?"

"Title? What's a title?" she asked with a much gentler shake of the head. "Who do you think I am?"

"Master Ruddick was very precise as to that," he said promptly. "You are the Master's most prized possession. And I am to treat you with the utmost care."

"What does 'utmost' mean?" she muttered under her breath.

"It means 'greatest'," Jasper replied. "He's just trying to use fancy words. He's being snooty. I doubt he's another of the priest's experimental slaves. Most likely he's just a hireling."

"Why does he keep staring at me like that?" she asked.

Kenneth quickly glanced over his shoulder with a slight look of panic. "Of whom do you speak, Mistress?"

"I was talking to Jasper, not you!"

"As you say, Mistress," Kenneth replied slowly.

"He thinks you're crazy," Jasper said. "And he's looking at you like that because he sexually attracted to you."

"I'm not crazy," she yelled at the new houseboy, then turned back to the hare. "What does that mean, 'sesualy atraciv'?"

"Pardon, Mistress?"

"It's pronounced 'sexually attractive'. It means he wants to have sex with you," the hare said.

"What's sex?"

The question made the young man's face bloom into a smile, and not a pleasant one. And on top of it he again gave off an aggressive feeling, like he badly wanted something. He strode toward her.

A panic seized her.

"Tell him if he takes another step Master Ruddick will hear of it," Jasper quickly instructed.

When she repeated the hare's words the man stopped and raised his hands. "I meant no offense, Mistress. I swear.

I was merely going to suggest you return to bed, and I will help you in doing so. That is all." He spoke quickly, "It is apparent that you need more rest. I shall have the cook bring you a meal and some milk to help you sleep. You are precious to the Master and we can't have anything happening to you."

He seemed to hear his own last words. His face turned slightly ashen, and the Girl felt his distress and uncertainty. After quickly excusing himself he left. She stuck her tongue out at the now closed door. She didn't like Kenneth, not one bit.

She crawled back into bed and lay down facing the hare. "What's going on, Jasper? Why is all this happening to me?"

"What's going on, is that the insane priest has apparently decided we need to spend much more time together. I'm guessing he thinks that if you can indeed talk to me then we should do so."

A thought sprung into her mind, one that made her afraid. But the hare spoke up, trying to belay her fears. "I am not the priest you encountered before. From what I see in your mind, that priest used an illusion to trick you. If I were just an illusion, I could not know your thoughts and speak to you through them."

The Girl had her doubts. After all that happened with Sam she didn't know what to believe. "How can you tell what I'm going to say before I say it?"

"Because we are connected through the True Tree," he said with a hint of awe.

"The what?" she asked.

"The True Tree. The first being, the creator of all existence. And somehow that bastard priest lucked upon a way to connect a human to it."

"I'm going to turn into a tree?" she exclaimed, tears forming in her eyes.

"You are not turning into a tree," he replied with forced patience. "The only thing you are turning into is an adult woman. That's the changes you are experiencing." He explained everything that was going to happen to her.

She didn't like it. "I'm going to start bleeding?"

"Didn't your mother tell you about any... Oh, I'm sorry. I didn't know." She felt him become embarrassed and quite sad for her. "Mothers are not supposed to do that to their children. You humans are strange, and with Chaos running the world at the moment you are even more so. It is past time that one relinquished his grip on the world."

"What does that mean?"

"Well, in the beginning, the True Tree created existence. It was a single plane that stretched into infinity."

"What's 'ifity'?"

"In-fin-i-ty. It means forever."

"Then why not just say that?"

"Hush now. I will get to that in a bit. It would appear that the priest did you right by placing me here. You've a lot to learn and I intend to teach you."

"How do you know so much?" she asked, fascinated.

"Because I, little one, am a direct descendant of the first spawned by the True Tree. I am no ordinary hare. I have been alive for over a thousand years. I spent much of my life within the Forest of Talendor acting as a messenger for the great Tebutarin king. Many Tebu's and Tebutarins of the Talendor can communicate with those of us who are derived of the Tree."

"How did you get here? And what's a Terbutatrin?"

Jasper audibly sighed. "Tebutarin are some of the first descendants of the Tree. Once they mature they never age. They are immortal." He sensed the questions that popped into her head. "Immortal means you can't die."

"So if they get a sword through their head, they won't die?"

"Of course they'd die from a sword to the head. I mean that they can't die of old age. It is a curse in a way. The only way a Tebutarin can die is through violence."

"But you said they were imratle."

"Immortal," he corrected. "Alright, so they're not truly immortal. Can I get on with the story? Where was I? Oh, yes. I happen to be in this unfortunate situation—"

"Unfor—"

"Bad place," he snapped. "I got in this 'bad place' because I was outside the Forest of Talendor when Chaos created the great prison that encompassed both the forest and the Durgian Empire—"

"The what?"

"I'll explain later," Jasper said with exasperation. "We've plenty of time."

He went on to tell her about the Great Game of the Gods won by the Lord of Chaos, and about how his reign should have ended before she'd been born.

"I was acting as a messenger from a group of Tebu in hiding."

"What was the message?" she asked.

"First, you need to learn to talk with only your mind."

"But how do I--" She closed her mouth and tried to think it but her brain was going too fast, too many thoughts and questions filled her mind.

"Okay, we'll put that aside for now," he remarked with a sigh. "You will learn. It is something you must learn because you don't want to go and tell that asshole priest everything."

"All right," she replied with a yawn.

Jasper didn't tell her the message but at that point she didn't care. He went on talking for quite a while. And before she fell asleep, she remembered an important question she needed to ask him.

"Jasper?"

"Yes, little one."

"What's sex?"

Sorrow's Heart   G. S. Scott

Chapter 6

Violation

The girl spent countless hours talking to Jasper. Whenever she wasn't doing her work about the house, sleeping, or undergoing one of Master Ruddick's sessions, she talked to and learned from the hare. Her taught her grammar, and expanded her vocabulary with words like, 'grammar' and 'vocabulary'.

"Can you teach me to read and write, too?" she asked him one evening as she sat before the hearth in her room, wrapped in a blanket and staring into the dancing flames. Her ability grew so she no longer needed to look at him to talk to him.

"I'm sorry, but I can't help you there, my dear," he said. "Reading and writing are about literacy."

"Literacy?" she asked, turning toward his cage. She wanted to hold him but the Master forbade it. He didn't want to take any chance in his escaping. The cage's lock was small but strong.

"Yes, honey," he said as he scratched at his ear with his foot. "Language and literacy are different. Language is about words, and a word is a way to organize and express thought. Literacy is when you translate those thought words into physical, communicable form. You see, we aren't speaking an actual language. We are merely broadcasting and reading each other's thoughts."

"So you understand the words when I speak them?" she asked. She found it all so confusing and fascinating.

"No, actually. I only understand the thoughts in your head. The sounds you make are nothing more than grunts and squawks to me." He shook his head violently, unable to rid himself of the itch.

"But you understand what Master Ruddick is saying." She reached her slim fingers through the bars of the cage and scratched his ear.

"Oh, thank you, my dear. That's wonderful," he groaned as she scratched. "No, I only understand the priest because I'm hearing him in your thoughts. It's rather like listening to him with your ears," Jasper replied. "Does that make any sense?"

"So when you're alone with him you don't understand anything he says?" She was disappointed. She hoped she might learn more of what he intended for her in the long run.

"No, I'm sorry." She felt his regret that he couldn't help her.

"Do you understand any other animals?" She moved her fingers to rub beneath his jaw.

"Only if they are also born of the True Tree." He stretched, relishing the rubbing. "Normal hares, and most other animals for that matter, communicate with noises and gestures like you humans and other sentient beings do. I communicate with normal hares in the same way. But if I meet a being of true spirit, a being of the direct bloodline of the first born of the True Tree, then I can speak as we are now."

"But that's not me," she muttered, stopping her stroking.

"That's why I am so amazed at what that crazy priest did to you. Through me he has somehow connected you to the spirit that flows from the Mother Tree."

"I thought you said it was the True Tree?"

She felt Jasper's amusement. "They are one and the same. The True Tree is often called the Mother Tree, or simply Mother."

She didn't like what that meant. "So he made me into a freak. Didn't he?" She wiped the tears forming in her eyes harshly, angry for letting even a small amount of sorrow show.

"You're not a freak," he said softly, rubbing his head on her fingers as they gripped the cage. "You are special. Truly special!" He paused. "I know how you feel about your own mother, but just know this." His thoughts filled with joy and wonder. "That crazy priest has unwittingly given you a new one, a mother of infinite wisdom and love. And Mother always looks after her own. You'll see."

The girl picked up Jasper's cage and walked to her bed. After lovingly placing the cage on her bedside table, she blew him a kiss and crawled into bed. Hunkering down in her bed she thought on what her friend told her until she fell asleep.

She tried her best to believe Jasper, but she couldn't shake her doubts. Doubts that turned even stronger as the days passed. Nothing seemed to get easier with the knowledge Jasper bestowed.

Master Ruddick visited her every day, wanting to see how well she was doing. And after a time his experimental sessions with her changed. He stopped using Jasper and worked with the other animals. Those sessions didn't hurt much, but they still made her feel uneasy. And with each passing session she even knew what they were thinking. She lamented at first, knowing Master Ruddick's experiments continued to change her, yet she latched on to what Jasper said, that she was now attached to a flow emanating from the True Tree, her Mother.

One afternoon, as she polished the dining room floor on her hands and knees, someone entered the room. By the lightness of the booted steps she knew it was Kenneth.

"And how are you this fine afternoon?" he asked blithely.

The girl immediately went on edge. Kenneth always tried to put forth an air of politeness but he was never this casual. She heard something else in his voice she didn't like, an air of impudence. She turned her head and saw his eyes staring at her backside. She felt his hunger.

"What do you want?" she asked tartly.

He smirked, "I just wanted to tell you that the Master will no longer be dining with anyone tonight."

Dorinda sent her to freshen up the room because Master Ruddick was expecting a young woman from the city of Selos. Usually when he took a woman for the night, it was someone from the local town. But this one seemed to be different somehow. "Does that mean I no longer have to do this?"

"Well, since you've started, you might as well finish," he said with a wave of his hand.

She turned and went back to her work but the houseboy didn't go. "Is there anything else?" she asked. He didn't answer, and several moments passed before she heard him turn and go.

Oh, how she hated Kenneth. Over time she learned he wasn't property, like she and the others. Instead he was something called a "freeman" in Master Ruddick's employ.

That night she awoke with a start. "Someone just came into the room," Jasper said. Fear rumbling in her belly, she peeked her head out from under the covers. The room held a distinct chill and the embers in the hearth cast a minimal amount of light. Even so, she could almost make out a shadowed figure standing at the door. Frantic, she tried to will Jasper to see more so she would know who it was.

The room lurched and spun about, and when her vision cleared, she saw far better than before. The light from the hearth shone far brighter, making the shadows about the room thinner. It felt odd, twisted and constrained. She also had a different perspective. But the strangest of all, she saw bars before her face.

The girl tried to look about and found she could not. She had no control over where she was looking. Terror rose in her throat.

"What's wrong?" Jasper asked anxiously.

Her vision spun about again and she found herself looking at... herself. "Oh dear gods, what's wrong with me now?"

"Is everything all right, my dearest?" Master Ruddick asked from the doorway, his voice almost a croon. "I didn't mean to frighten you."

Her vision spun again until she was looking about with her own eyes once more. "Something just happened," she stammered. Without thinking she blurted out the experience.

"Truly?" Elation filled his voice. "So you can now see through the rodent's eyes as well. Excellent."

A ball of softly glowing light appeared above his outstretched hand. The light glowed of every color imaginable, spinning about the ball frantically. Its eerie light bathed her Master's face, giving him a surreal expression. He approached her bed, pausing a moment to look at Jasper, then sat on the edge of her bed.

"Is there something you need of me, Master?" she squeaked. He'd not done this before, and it filled her with unease.

"No, I just came here to have a look at you," he said, his voice slightly slurred.

"He's drunk," Jasper said. "And by the smell of it I'd say on brandy."

Master Ruddick gently reached out and touched her hair, caressing it. He then moved his hand to her shoulder, lightly stroking and squeezing it before it slid down her arm until he held her hand.

Her skin prickled and her stomach clenched. It was the same kind of thing Samuel had done. She felt something in his mind that she didn't like. His hunger blazed, tempered with a mixture of pride and, oddly enough, a great deal of caring. Could he genuinely cherish her?

"You cannot trust him," Jasper said. "His kind are twisted. You know this!"

"But I think he loves me," she mentally replied. "I don't know how I never saw it before."

"That's not love! He 'cherishes' you because he owns you. You are his most prized possession." Jasper's thoughts turned anxious. "And I fear he is about to abuse you, terribly."

"What do you want of me—"

She squealed as her covers were flung to the floor.

"No need to fear, my sweet thing," Master Ruddick soothed as he tightened his grip on her hand while moving his other to the back of her neck. "This is merely how we show appreciation. And I do so appreciate all the accomplishments you've made."

He pulled her to him and pressed his lips onto hers. His breath smelled of brandy and onions and it made her gag.

The Master didn't seem to notice or care. He pulled his head back. "Your skin is so soft and supple. You're growing into a beautiful young woman." He moved the hand from behind her head and placed it upon her growing bosom. "Yes, one day these will be quite lovely."

"As you say, Master." She slowly tried to pull away.

A spike of anger flaired within him. "And just where do you think you're going? You women are all alike," he said in a low voice and he looked over her head. "I'm not worth her time, am I? Well, there are far finer things in this world than that prig!"

The girl had no idea what he was talking about and his grip tightened. "Master, you're hurting me."

His anger went white hot. "So what if I am? You are mine to do with as I please." His snarling face changed into one with a wicked, half smile. "Or have you forgotten that? Perhaps I've been too soft on you of late."

He yanked her to an inch from his face. "It's time you learned a lesson." His spittle spraying her face. He threw her back onto the bed, stood, and tore open his robe.

"Close your eyes, sweetheart," Jasper said softly. "Don't look." She did as her one and only friend told her.

Master Ruddick spun her about, face down, and then pulled her until her legs hung off the bed. She heard him spit. Then she felt only pain. It was not the same as during the experiments where her mind felt as though it were being sliced with knives. Nor did it feel like her entire body was being ripped apart over and over again. No, this pain was far more localized. It pierced and tore her, wrenching her gut. It hurt so bad she wanted to do something she'd promised herself to never do again. But she refused to cry.

When the pain stopped, when the Master's horrific defiling ended, she was in a state of stunned silence. She was numb. She wanted to curl into a ball and sleep, sleep and never awaken.

"It's all over, honey," Jasper whispered.

But she didn't want to hear it. All his silly talk about "Mother loving her" and "Mother will take care of her," rang hollow in her ears. He tried to console her more, but she shut him out.

Master Ruddick laid a hand upon her back and gently patted it. "I'm sorry, my precious," he said softly.

He gingerly picked up her legs and placed them upon the bed, turning her onto her side. She couldn't help but look at him. Wave after wave of regret, pain, self-loathing, and remorse oozed from the Master. "You deserve better than that. I am truly sorry. I shall have the cook come right away and bathe you."

She stared down at her blood soaked nethers, but felt nothing.

On his way out he said one last thing to her before closing the door, "Do not worry, my precious little one. This will never happen again."

But he lied.

Chapter 7

Presentable

The girl refused to forgive Jasper for filling her mind with lies about a loving mother who looked after her. Jasper begged her to listen to reason, he begged her to not shut him out. But she did anyway. She hated him. She hated Master Ruddick, and Dorinda, and Kos, and Kenneth. She hated everyone in the entire world. But mostly she hated herself.

After that horrific night, the girl withdrew back in on herself once more. She couldn't get out of bed the first few days, the pain left her nearly immobile. But after that she refused to leave her bed. She found something new deep within herself and she latched hold. Her obstinacy gave her strength. In the end, Dorinda stopped bringing her food and milk, so she was forced to get up.

After gingerly putting on her loosest fitting dress, she snuck out of her room and stole into the kitchen. Keeping an eye out for the cook, she quickly grabbed a loaf of bread cooling on the table. However, halfway back to her room, Kenneth spotted her.

"Back among the living, are we?" he asked.

She didn't bother answering him, she simply bolted for her room. She didn't make it. The houseboy ran her down and knocked her to the floor.

"Get up," he scolded her. "You've got work to do. I'm done doing your share."

With a growl the girl sprung to her feet and threw herself at the boy, catching him by surprise. They tumbled to the floor with her on top. She then pummeled the boy about the face and chest, screaming at the top of her lungs.

Dorinda arrived to pull the girl off the bloody faced houseboy as Master Ruddick came storming down the steps.

He stared at the girl as she kicked and struggled in the cook's grasp. She even bit the cook's hand.

"So you want to revert to an animal?" the Master said. "So be it."

He quickly wrapped the girl in a cocoon of Chaos, the pure essence of the Lord of Chaos. No matter how hard the girl struggled she could not break free. She screamed and snarled and spit. It made no difference. He dragged her through the house and down into the basement. Master Ruddick flung open her old cage door and shoved her inside. Once he locked the door, he released her from the cocoon.

"You will stay down here with the animals until such a time as you stop acting like one of them." He paused a moment and said softly, "Perhaps I have gone too far with you. There is a chance our sessions have pushed you too far and you've garnered their nature as you gain their thoughts. Either way you shall stay here until I think you will become useful to me once again." The Master stripped off her dress, tearing it to pieces, and walked back upstairs.

She slammed her fists against the bars in frustration then sat back into the straw, nursing her bruised arms. She hated being back in the cage! She angrily wiped away the tears that continuously threatened to spring from her eyes. She would not cry! Never again! They did not deserve her tears.

"This one has dragon fire in its veins," said a voice blossoming into her mind. It wasn't Jasper's voice, it was much too strong.

She eyed the cage against the other wall, the very cage that held countless frightened and tortured children. Within the cage sat a large, black wolf gazing back at her, its bright yellow eyes seeming to glow. She turned her back on it and crawled to the very back of the cage and burrowed under the straw.

She found sleep difficult. The straw scratched her, insects infested the cage, and it stank. She had grown accustomed to more than just sleeping in a bed. She had forgotten the smell. The thick, pungent stink, a mixture of animal musk, dampness, mold, urine, and feces made her want to gag.

She shut the wolf out of her mind after it spoke to her but she could still feel it. It lurked, like a predator waiting to pounce upon its prey. She poked her head above the straw and looked over at its cage. The wolf now lay at the back of its cage yet she saw its eyes still on her. She buried herself once more but still she felt it. Its presence was ominous.

Master Ruddick left her in the basement for three days before coming to see her. Her anger still flared high and the sight of him made her hackles rise. Just the look of him reminded her of what he had done. The pain and humiliation... She wanted to kill him.

She felt a mixture of emotions raging through him. A mixture of ownership, uncertainty, and regret. It made no sense to her. Then again, she didn't care. She refused to say anything and simply stared at him until he left.

She spent another week in that cage. Unlike before she wasn't let out to do house work, and the confines grew suffocating. Her skin became covered with rashes and she always shivered from the cold. They didn't change her straw and her refuse not taken away. Dorinda still fed her but nothing more than bread and water once in the morning and once at night.

When Kos came down to feed the animals, she felt his stares. She did her best to ignore them. On his way out he threw a large chunk of meat into the wolf's cage. He then turned and looked at her once more.

"I knew you'd end up back down here," he said with a sneer. "Perhaps I'll come back later and keep you warm." His chuckle sent a chill down her spine and his hunger for her was nearly ravenous. He left without another word.

As she lay there, she smelled the wolf's meat. It made her stomach growl. She watched as the wolf approached and sniffed it. He didn't gobble it down like she would have. Instead he just sat down and glared at it. She felt his disdain when he finally ate. Once finished he laid back down and continued to stare at her. She saw an intelligence behind those eyes. He was no ordinary wolf.

She considered opening her mind and talking to him but thought better of it. He would probably tell her more things that turned out to be lies. Or perhaps he'd simply regale her with visions of how he'd stalk and eat her. So she buried herself beneath the straw and tried to sleep.

She awoke with a start when someone rapped on her cage. Terrified, she thought it was Kos, come to make good on his threat. But it was Master Ruddick.

"Are you ready to act like something more than an animal, or has your stay down here solidified you in a feral state?"

The girl felt confused. Without Jasper there to help her with some of Master Ruddick's words, she wasn't sure what to say. What was a 'feral'? If she answered wrong, she feared he would indeed leave her in the cage for the rest of her life.

"No answer? So be it." He turned and walked away.

She flung herself at the bars of the cage, her arms reaching through trying to grasp the Master's robes. "No, Master! Please don't leave me here! I'll be better, I swear."

He stopped and turned his head to look at her. "Truly?"

"Yes, Master, I swear." She couldn't take being down there anymore. It was all getting to her—the stink, the itching, Kos, and especially the wolf. "Please, Master! I will be good!"

Yet Master Ruddick left anyway. She sunk down into the straw, distraught. She wrapped her arms about herself and trembled. What would happen to her now, she wondered. When she looked up at the wolf it grinned.

A few moments later she heard footsteps on the stairs once more. It was Dorinda. She approached her cage, bent down, and blessedly unlocked the door. When she swung it open, she held out her hand. "Come now, little one. The Master bade me to get you cleaned up and properly fed." As the girl headed to the door, the cook pulled her hand back. "You promise not to bite me again?"

Nodding, she accepted Dorinda's hand and left the cage. She then flung herself at the cook's legs and hugged her with all her might. It took a moment for Dorinda to unwrap the girl's arms. She took the girl by the hand and they walked up the stairs. The girl felt the wolf's eyes on her every step she took.

The morning light through the window bathed the girl in its wonderful warmth. She'd been thoroughly scrubbed, her rashes covered in some kind of floral scented cream, and her hair washed. She felt worlds better. Yet deep down, she couldn't help but feel as though she had failed. In the end, her stubbornness failed her, and she was no better off than before.

Her dreams the next night were odd. A strange tint covered everything, and they were rather frenetic. She ran or stalked through forests and open fields, swam through ponds, and wallowed in mud puddles. She played and roughhoused with her brothers and sisters.

She knew the dreams belonged the wolf as she had done none of those things in her life. The dreams made her feel happy upon awakening, but that quickly turned to sorrow. She never knew such things were possible, and she never would.

As she sat up and stretched, she was surprised Jasper's cage was not on the night stand. She had been far too tired the night before to even notice him gone. She couldn't decide if it was a good thing or a bad.

She padded over to her wash table and mirror. She picked up the cake of soap and eyed herself in the mirror. Her hair was a wild tangled mess. She didn't hate what she saw, in fact she rather liked it. She stood there trying to imagine how she looked before the bath the night before. Going by the amount of grime that filled the tub when she got out she must have been all soot and dirt. The thought made her smile. The Master wanted her to be all clean and presentable. But deep down she still wanted to rebel. She felt happy that her stubbornness still lingered to give her strength. She knew she needed it. She put on one of her work dresses and slippers and left her room.

As she walked down the stairs to the ground floor, she saw Kenneth dusting one of the dark, wooden tables near the door. As she descended, his face split into a smirk. "I hope you learned your lesson, little animal," he quipped.

She didn't like being called an animal. When Master Ruddick said he thought she might become one of his animals, the idea terrified her. She would not let that happen, no matter what! She dearly wanted to race over to him and punch him.

He's not worth it, she thought. He is a little boy in a large world and when the time comes, he will find himself all alone. He'll be prey for the pack.

The thought brought her up short. The wolf's dreams must still affect her, clouding her vocabulary. She shook her head, and when she reached the bottom of the stairs she ignored him, making her way to the kitchen.

"How are you feeling this morning?" Dorinda asked as she entered.

"I am well, thank you," she replied, trying to sound sweet and innocent. By the expression on the cook's face she didn't pull it off.

"All right, my little hellion," Dorinda said with a cheerful smile. "You have your breakfast and then it's off to housework for you."

The girl smiled, liking the sound of hellion. She wolfed down her breakfast of eggs, bacon, bread, and ewe's milk. After wiping her mouth with the back of her hand, she thanked the cook with a smile. Dorinda gave her a short list of work that needed doing, which mostly involved the main dining chamber. The list's brevity surprised her.

"Now I need you to do all those things promptly, you understand?" the cook said before the girl headed out the door. "The Master is having several guests coming in the afternoon and he wants that room presentable. You are then to go to your room and clean yourself and put on your best dress. He wants you to be presentable as well."

The girl didn't like the sound of that.

Chapter 8

The Dinner

Master Ruddick sat at the head of the table. He wore light blue robes and a gold sash, with his long black hair tied at the back of his neck with a multicolored cloth that twisted the entire length.

Four other people sat about the table deep in conversation, three men and one woman. The three men wore robes of different colors—one yellow, one brown, and one blue—and the woman wore a white shirt and blue breeches. They all had dark hair, but the Girl didn't see much more as she kept her gaze down.

She helped Dorinda serve the food consisting of pork and lamb with three different types of greens and some golden squash. The platters were large, but she handled them with not too much of a problem. Dorinda poured them all their drinks, two wanting brandy, and the rest wanting wine. As the Girl turned to leave with the cook, Master Ruddick called out to her.

"Stop, my dear. Come here." He waved a hand indicating he wanted her to stand at his side. "Dorinda, tell Kenneth he is to come in now."

The Girl hesitated only a moment before hurrying to the Master's side. She had no idea what was going on. Initially she was relieved when the cook told her she needed to dress presentably because she would help to serve the guests. But now that the Master waved her over she knew it was going to be much more.

She tried not to fidget. She wore her finest dress, which was pale blue with gold ruffles hanging past her knees. It tied in the front with short ruffled sleeves and ribbons that Dorinda needed to help her tie. She deathly feared to get any of it dirty. Even her slippers were made of satin with little bows on them. Dorinda also tied ribbons in her hair after brushing until it shone. The Girl felt so uncomfortable.

"Yes, Master," she said softly as she reached his side.

"And who is this lovely little thing?" the woman asked in a high, yet soft voice.

"This is my most prized possession. And she is the reason I've asked you all here tonight," Master Ruddick said with pride.

"Truly?" asked one of the men. The Girl peeped at him. He wore yellow robes and had sparse facial hair. "Is she for sale?" He had a predatory look in his dark eyes.

"Hardly," Master Ruddick replied with a wave of his hand.

"We all know you've gone through scores of children," remarked the man in blue. "What makes this one worth showing?"

Master Ruddick took a finger and raised her chin so she looked at him. She shivered. "I want you to do something for me," he said to her softly, yet loud enough to be heard by the room. "I want you to show these people what you can now do."

She glanced at the people about the table then back to the Master. She swallowed hard and nodded. She understood none of this. The Master then called out to Kenneth who promptly entered holding Jasper's cage.

The moment she looked at the hare her anger rose. The Master told her to do this, but she felt obstinate. She felt Jasper's thoughts yet she had difficulty lowering her guard. She really didn't want to let him in again.

"Go on, child," Master Ruddick prompted. "Show them."

"I don't—"

"You don't what?" he barked. "You will do as you're told. I'll have no more of this tomfoolery."

Still, the Girl hesitated. She feared if she let Jasper in again he would fill her head with more lies. The pain Master Ruddick put her through was bad enough, but to let Jasper try and convince her that she could be anything more than she was... She couldn't do that.

"Do it, I said," the Master yelled.

"Honestly, Ruddick. I appreciate the lovely meal but I've better things to do than sit here and watch you berate a slave," said the man in brown. "Everyone knows how you seem to enjoy slaughtering children. The Lord knows your veracity has rivaled even that of the Cleansing. But to what end? To prove you can make a filthy peasant look presentable?"

Master Ruddick didn't reply. He simply stared harder at the Girl for a moment before turning to the houseboy and giving him a nod. To the Girl's horror she saw Kenneth draw a long, slim dagger and stick it through the bars of the cage. Jasper panicked. She felt his thoughts even stronger, begging her to listen. She felt the point of the dagger pierce his skin.

"No," she screamed. "Please, don't! I'll do it, I swear." She opened her mind up to Jasper.

"Please, you can't let them do this," Jasper implored. "Why are they doing this? What's going on?"

"I'm sorry, Jasper," she said out loud. She still had difficulty only speaking with her mind. "They want to prove I can talk to you." She turned to Master Ruddick. "He's scared and wants to know what's going on!"

"What is this?" the man in yellow asked. "Did you bring us here to see some kind of mummer's farce?"

"No, I can do it. I swear," the Girl told the man. She turned back to Jasper. "Talk to me. Tell me something so they understand."

"I've had enough of this," snapped the man in yellow and he began to stand.

"Wait," the woman said. "I can see it. I can see a flow between the child and the animal. It's faint, but it is there."

"Continue, sweetheart," Master Ruddick said.

"Jasper," the Girl implored, "just tell me anything."

"Child," the man in brown said, "make it tell you something only it would know about."

"Tell them where I am from," Jasper said, "but do not tell them I am a courier for the Tebus or about Mother. That could prove disastrous."

She became irked about his mentioning of his so called "Mother" again but she did as he asked. She told the people he hailed from the Talendor forest to the north. She conveyed information about the trees and animals, things she simply could not know.

In the end the three men left still unconvinced, but the woman stayed on a bit longer, having the Girl ask Jasper question after question. Most of them made no sense, but she asked, anyway.

By evenings end the Girl stood at her Master's side at the front door. The dark haired woman, awaiting her coach, pulled up the hood of her cloak as a gentle rain fell. A gust of wind whipped through the open door, giving the Girl a chill. For the first time she regretted not wearing her stockings.

"It really is quite fascinating," the dark haired woman said to the Girl's Master. "There was most certainly a connection between them. Whether she was simply making things up it's hard to tell. I know next to nothing about the north, but she certainly seems to believe it. And you say that it was much stronger before?"

"Yes," Master Ruddick replied, "considerably so. I can only surmise that either it now requires less of the Lord's Breath or her connection to the animal is flagging."

The Girl kept wondering what they were talking about. What did someone's breath have to do with it? she thought.

"It is the name they use for their manipulation of the direct power of the Lord of Chaos," Jasper said. "It's a bit pompous if you ask—"

She shut him out of her mind, sharply. It surprised her she could even still hear him. Kenneth had taken him away when they finished dinner and she didn't know exactly where to.

"Are you sure I can't convince you to spend the night?" Master Ruddick asked the woman as her carriage pulled up before the door.

The woman smiled, her green eyes sparkling in the lighted foyer. The woman was quite pretty. The Girl had been so scared during the dinner she hadn't noticed.

The Girl felt the woman contemplate the invitation for a moment. "Perhaps another time, Ruddick. I have much to consider." The woman gave the Master a slight nod and walked out the door.

"Come, my little one," Master Ruddick said after the woman's carriage pulled away. He gently placed his hand upon her shoulder and guided her toward the back of the manor. "You deserve a treat for your work this evening."

Once in the kitchen he told Dorinda to give her a sweet cake especially made for her. The Girl hadn't even heard of such a thing, let alone tasted one before. She found it heavenly. It filled both her hands and took her several minutes to finish.

As she licked her hands of the sweet stickiness left behind, Master Ruddick knelt before her and took her chin in his hand. "You were wonderful today. But Celeste is right. We must find out why the connection is thinning."

The Girl certainly didn't like the sound of that. The Master then stood and asked Dorinda for a bottle of brandy. "Make sure she gets to bed right away," he told the cook. "She will need to be well rested for tomorrow."

The cook nodded at the Master, but as he turned his back the woman frowned slightly. She turned and walked to a cupboard, pulling out a small porcelain canister. She took a pinch of whatever it contained and dropped it into a cup, then filled the cup with ewe's milk.

"Come now, my sweet," the cook said, her voice sweet, but she oozed concern. "Let's get you into bed. This will help wash away the excess sweetness. We wouldn't want you to get a tummy ache now."

She ushered the Girl into the hallway and off to her room. Once there, she helped the Girl into her nightshirt then into bed. As Dorinda tucked the Girl in she gave her the milk. "Now you drink this up. By the look in your eye I'm guessing you are going to have trouble sleeping tonight so I put a little something in there to help."

Once the Girl finished drinking, Dorinda retrieved the cup. She took a long look at the Girl, her eyes seeming as sad as ever. "Sleep well, little one," she murmured and left, quietly closing the door.

Jasper wasn't there, which suited The Girl fine. She rolled over onto her side and felt herself slip quickly into sleep.

The Girl groggily opened her eyes to the dark room. She didn't know what woke her but something didn't feel right. Something moved within the room. A terror rose within her but she was too lethargic to move.

"Damn you, bitch. Why wouldn't you just stay?" Master Ruddick said.

The Girl, now in a full blown panic, tried to get up but failed, her voice came out as little more than a squeak. Her eyes burned when a bright light formed above her Master, who wore not a stitch. He appeared both sad and angry… but mostly hungry.

The Girl blessedly did not remember much more. Whatever Dorinda gave her had seen to that. When the cook came to her room in the morning with her breakfast, it was plain on her face she knew what had transpired. She told the Girl she needn't worry about her duties that day and to get some rest. But the following day she needed to be ready to go back to work.

She slept on and off throughout the day. The Master did not come and see her, only Dorinda. The cook asked if she wanted her hare but the Girl rejected the idea. The previous night was just more proof of Jasper's lies.

The following day she got up early and started her day's work. Kenneth told her what needed doing, and she got about it without another word. At around midday Master Ruddick came to her and told her he needed her in the basement. She bit her lip to keep herself from crying.

With each step into that dank, dark place she felt the walls start to close in. The air felt heavy and her throat felt tight. As she neared the door into the basement, she saw the wolf in his cage, staring at her. He didn't try and talk to her. He merely stared, his yellow eyes meeting hers. She had this overwhelming sense he was biding his time. To what extent she didn't know beyond that it would be bad.

Master Ruddick sat the Girl on the stool next to his workbench, on which Jasper's cage sat. "You don't need to worry about your dress," he told her. "This should be very easy. I simply want to see what is going on with your connection to your friend, Jasper."

"He's not my friend," she muttered under her breath. When he asked her what she said she simply lowered her head.

"Just sit still," he snapped.

She felt the Master's unease when he addressed her. He bore the same regret and remorse as the last time, only less sharp. She feared it was not a good thing.

Master Ruddick closed his eyes a moment and lightly gestured with his hands. Once he opened them he glanced at Jasper and then at her. The Girl felt her skin become covered with goose bumps.

"All right, now I want you to talk with him," he said softly. "And I'll brook no nonsense. You got me?"

"Yes, Master," she replied, meekly. And she felt meek, too, to her own sorrow. Where had her fire gone? What happened to her stubbornness?

She looked up at Jasper and once again became angry. "Why did you do this to me," she asked Jasper bitterly. "Why did you ever tell me those lies?"

"I didn't lie to you, I swear," he said, his voice full of hurt and dejection.

"How dare you say that!" she shouted. "How dare you sit there and—"

Her mind exploded in pain. The world spun about her wildly and she thought her entire body was on fire. She felt herself lose control of her bodily functions before she passed out.

"That man truly is a fool," a voice said softly in her mind.

She opened her eyes and looked about her. She lay in the basement bed, next to the fire. She guessed something must have gone wrong as the Master told her it would not hurt. She cursed herself. That's what she got for believing what anyone told her. Oh how she wished him dead!

"There's that fire," the voice said. "You needn't worry about losing that, little one. That dragon's blood runs strong in you."

She realized with a shock that it was the wolf talking to her. In her dulled state she thought it had been Jasper. "Why are you taunting me?"

"I do not taunt, little cub," it replied. "It is merely an observation."

She felt its amusement on the far side of the room. "Why did you call Master a fool?"

"Because he is one," the wolf said. "He has no idea what he's doing, and he's just trying to repeat his earlier unexpected success. The problem is he can't. And in the process he's just hurting the two of you."

"He hurt Jasper, too?"

"Jasper?" the wolf chuckled. "I should have expected such a name for the likes of him. Yes, he hurt the hare the same time he hurt you, and then took him upstairs after seeing to you."

"Jasper's a fine name," she snapped. "I bet you don't even have one." But she got no response from the wolf, just a sudden feeling of alertness.

"Oh, but you already know my name, my little morsel," came a cruel voice from the darkness of the stairs.

"Kos!" Terror ripped through her body. After their last encounter she hoped to never see him again. Yet there he was, alone in the basement with her. Only this time she wasn't safe within her cage.

"Yes, it's your dear friend, Kos," the stableman said as he came into view. The light of the fire played across his face making him look demonic.

"What do you want?" She tried to burrow deeper into the covers.

"You know what I want," he replied with a sneer. "And by the looks of it you're no longer in the Master's graces. I hear tell he's already deflowered you." Kos slowly approached the Girl. "I'm sure he won't mind if I have a piece as well."

He stopped next to her bed and dragged back her covers. To her own remorse she lay naked beneath. She tried to struggle but had no strength. She thought her only hope was Dorinda might hear her if she screamed.

Kos slapped a hand across her mouth. "Now, now. I'll have none of that," he said while with his other hand he loosened the drawstrings on his trousers.

Her mind flailed and cried out, causing the animals to become agitated. They thrashed about in their cages, squealing and chittering. Yet the Girl knew it would do little good. They often made noise and they could not be heard upstairs.

Once Kos lowered his pants, he kicked them away and used his free hand to grab one of her legs and turn her toward him. He licked his lips, nearly causing her to vomit. She kicked out at him with her free leg but she was still too weak to do anything other than make the man chuckle.

"That's it! I love it when they put up at least a little bit of a fight." He placed one knee on the bed and tried to align himself. "Don't worry, you're gonna love—"

Kos let out a scream and flew up into the air, crashing into the ceiling, and then falling on the floor with a dull thud next to her bed. He lay there and groaned.

The Girl saw movement out of the corner of her eye, a dark shadow in the basement doorway. The Girl shivered.

The shadow slowly came closer and closer until it revealed itself to be Master Ruddick.

"Just what do you think you're doing?" Ruddick questioned in a hard, cold voice. "She's not community property. She's my property." He then tilted his head slightly to the side. "As are you."

Kos rose back into the air and hung there a moment before he threw his head back and shrieked. The screams grew bloodcurdling as the Girl saw the man's genitals catch fire. He howled in anguish as his legs melted, then his arms.

"I don't like it when other people touch my things," Master Ruddick said quietly.

The wailing, deformed man then flew into the large fireplace, and burst into flames. She felt a huge gust of wind flow from the stairway and into the hearth where the fire grew hotter and hotter. It grew so hot the Girl weakly raised up her arm to cover her face. After several minutes the wind ceased, and the fire died down. Nothing remained of Kos in the hearth, not even ash.

"It would appear that I need a new stableman," Master Ruddick said calmly. He leaned over and gently kissed the Girl on the forehead. "I'll have Dorinda bring you down something to make sure you sleep. You need your rest." He turned and headed for the stairs. In the darkness she heard him say, "I'll never let anything happen to you."

Sorrow's Heart   G. S. Scott

Chapter 9

Casandra

She awoke in her own bed. Sunlight streamed through the window illuminating dust motes in the air. She felt weak, so she slowly sat up. Her head swam as she looked about the room and saw that Master Ruddick had returned Jasper's cage. At first the Girl wasn't sure what she should do about it. The Master obviously wanted her to go back to talking with the hare but she had difficulty letting go of her anger.

"I'm still mad at you, you know," the Girl said to the hare.

"I understand you're mad," Jasper replied anxiously. "But I just wish you would see that Mother—"

She cut him off viciously. "No! I don't want to hear it! What don't you get about that?" She couldn't believe that he immediately went back to that. "No more talk about mothers. All they do is lie to you and turn their backs on you."

"All right, all right, I'm sorry," Jasper capitulated. A moment of silence passed between them before the hare added, "I'm glad the priest got to you in time last night. I was so worried."

"Me too," she replied.

She still saw it in her mind, Kos about to do disgusting, unthinkable things to her and suddenly there stood a man she hated to her very core, with a wild look in his eye. Her savior? She loathed him and yet at that moment she had never been happier to see anyone in her life. It sent a flutter into her stomach she didn't understand.

"How did he even know I was in trouble?" she wondered out loud.

"I told him," Jasper said.

"How?"

"Well, he had me in his room, casually inspecting me. When I felt your distress I just panicked and ran around my cage," Jasper said. "He must have figured out something was wrong with you."

"He really cares about me, doesn't he?" she asked, her mind filled with confusion.

"No!" Jasper retorted. "You are an investment to him, nothing more."

"That's not true," she shouted back. "If that's all I am to him he wouldn't have cared what Kos did to me. Not like that anyway."

"I'm telling you—"

"That's enough! No more," she shouted and shut him out of her mind once more.

The hare hissed and thumped in his cage but the Girl didn't care. She hastily dragged herself out of bed and fell to the floor after only a couple of steps. She still had no strength after the previous night's session with the Master. Crawling back to the bed she pulled herself to her feet with the sheets. Once steady enough, she slowly made her way to the armoire and pulled out one of her working dresses and slippers. After donning them she hastened to the door, nearly falling twice. Once outside she slammed the door. And promptly fell.

"What is the meaning of this?" Master Ruddick asked behind her. He swiftly came to her side and helped her to her feet. "You can hardly walk. What do you think you're doing getting out of bed in your condition?"

She blurted out how Jasper had angered her and the statement he made about the Master not really caring about her. She immediately wanted to take it back.

"Did he now?" Master Ruddick mused. "It just may be time I rid myself of him."

"No, no," she pleaded. "Please don't do that. I didn't mean it. I take it back. Please don't kill him!"

"Kill him?" he said with a laugh. "I would hardly do that. He's far too valuable. But I do know someone who might be interested in a trade."

"No, please don't," she begged.

He continued on, ignoring her pleas. "Yes, Geoff has a fine pair of stablemen. I'm sure he'd be willing to trade me one for the hare." He shook his head at her continued begging. "My dear. You are not listening. I've already decided. You know I now need someone to work the stables." He then paused and looked at her with a subtle smile on his face. "Unless of course I found someone else who would be willing to do the work for a while."

That brought her up short. "Do you… do you mean me, Master?"

His smile grew broad. "I knew you were an exceptionally bright one. The Great Lord has blessed you in so many ways. Yes, my sweet, precious one. I'm saying that I would like you to work with the horses for me."

She trembled. The idea of going outside terrified her. Many times, she gazed out the window at the trees and the sky, admiring its beauty. But it was quite different to even think of actually going out there. She could still see the look on Andik's face.

"But I'll die," she whimpered.

"Nonsense," he replied with a shake of his head. "I told you, I will never let any harm come to you. You are my precious one." He gently ran his thumb over her cheek. He took her by the hand and led her toward the stairs. "Come, let me show you."

Once at the central stairway, the Master picked her up and carried her in his arms as her legs still lacked the strength to descend the stairs herself. It was an unusual feeling for her–she felt warm and safe cradled in his arms. She gazed at him and he smiled back at her. She couldn't decide if Jasper had lied to her or not about Master Ruddick.

As they headed down the hall toward the kitchen, the Girl fidgeted. The Master was not slowing, and each step was like a tread of doom. When they entered the kitchen, surprise filled Dorinda's face, particularly when the Master asked her to get the door for him.

The cook opened the door and stepped out to make room for them. The Girl did more than fidget, she struggled. She pictured Andik's face as he ran out that door, the look of pain and horror as he turned red and clawed at his throat. She didn't want to die like that.

"Please, Master, no. I will be good, I swear," she pleaded as she struggled. "Please, Master, I don't want to die!"

Master Ruddick stepped out into the stable yard without a word. He held her tightly to him and stopped a few feet out the door. She screamed and kicked, just waiting for her throat to close and her eyes to bulge… but nothing happened.

"Shh," he cooed to her, gently rocking her in his arms. "See? You're all right."

Her breaths came in heavy pants and she glanced about wildly. Minutes passed and her breath slowed. She marveled at smiling face, and how his eyes sparkled in the sunlight.

"Dorinda," he said to the cook, "bring me a good chair so we can sit here for a while. She still needs to regain her strength and get her bearings."

He took the seat Dorinda brought for him and simply sat there holding the Girl, on his lap, his arms tightly about her.

They sat there for several hours as the Girl's strength returned. She looked all about the stable yard and beyond. She watched the sparse clouds dance in the sky and the trees sway in the light wind that played across her skin and flowed through her hair. The wonderful warmth of the sun baithed her face. Everything smelled crisp and clean. It was amazing.

"Let's see if you can keep your feet, shall we?" The Master lowered her off his lap.

Her slippered feet touched the grass, and she stood. She could hardly believe it, being outside. When she took a few tentative steps, she felt fine. She wanted to run. Not to run away, but simply run for the sake of running.

"Thank you, Master," she said, her voice choking up. She headed for the stables but stopped and glanced back. Master Ruddick, still sitting, just gazed at her, smiling. So she waited for him.

After a few moments Master Ruddick stood and led her to the stables. He pushed aside one of the doors with a bit of a grunt. "I will have Dorinda put something on these so you will be able to do this yourself."

As she stepped in, smells she never knew assaulted her senses. She knew the smell of hay of course but everything else was different. The smells of the dust and the animals themselves seemed far cleaner than the damp and mustiness of the basement. It smelled dry and light.

"Come here, my little one," he called as he beckoned her to where he stood by a stall. "I've two horses and you will need to curry them along with getting them food and water every day."

She stared at the huge chestnut colored horse in the stall. It intimidated her. "What's its name?" she asked. She decided if they had names they wouldn't seem as menacing.

"I've no idea," he said as though the thought never occurred to him. He looked at her, his face still smiling, and placed his hand atop her head. "You name them, my dear."

The Girl eyed the horse. "Is this one a boy or a girl?"

"This one is a mare," he replied, nodding to the horse before them. "The dappled gray is a gelding." He saw the confusion on her face and laughed. "A mare is a girl horse, and a gelding is a boy, or at least he used to be one."

The Girl had no idea what the Master's last statement meant, but she nodded, regardless. "The boy horse's name will be Wind, because I like the wind," she said with a smile. But her smile quickly turned to a frown without realizing it. The mare felt rather sad; its eyes held a bleak and despondent look. "The girl horse's name is Casandra."

Master Ruddick looked at her queerly. "Why that name?"

The Girl shook her head, "I don't know."

"Did she tell you that name?"

"No," she shook her head. "She's not that smart, not like Jasper or—" She stopped. She didn't want the Master to know the wolf could talk to her like Jasper. She didn't really like the wolf, it scared her, but for some reason she kept it to herself.

"Then why name it Casandra?"

"I don't know. It just popped into my head, like I heard it someplace before." The name made her frown more.

She gazed deeper into the horse and saw something that made her angry. "Kos used to beat her. When she didn't want to do something he would whip her."

The Master patted her on the head. "Well, she doesn't have to worry about that anymore, now does she?"

The Girl beamed. "What does 'curry' mean?"

"It means you brush it." He opened the gate to its stall. "Here, let me show you." The Master then entered, waving to her to follow. He picked up a brush sitting on a shelf and brushed the horse. "Here, you do it." After handing her the brush he pulled up a stool.

Sensing the horse's uneasiness she was tentative at first. She gazed into its eyes and told it everything would be all right.

Casandra was shocked at first that the Girl talked to her in a way she could understand, but quickly accepted it. As the Girl brushed, she told Casandra about Kos not being there anymore and she would look after them for a while. Casandra whinnied and pawed at the ground happily.

As the day progressed the Master showed her how to bridle the horses and walked them about the stable yard. Casandra enjoyed every moment of it and Wind, who was at first uncertain, grew to relish their session. His wild spirit dearly preferred running over walking, but he still enjoyed just being outside. Apparently Kos didn't exercise them as he should have.

Dusk grew when the Master said it was time to put the horses away and head back inside. "Come," he placed his hand upon her head, "we will eat together in the dining room and then it's off to bed with you."

The dinner of glazed pork, beans, and squash was strange to the Girl. She'd never eaten at that table and certainly not with Master Ruddick. He kept looking at her with his mixed feelings. The possessiveness and pride shone brightly, but behind it lay the hunger mixed with his fading feeling of guilt.

When she walked to her room that night Jasper's cage was gone, leaving her conflicted. She seemed to feel that way about a great many things as of late. She was glad to see him gone. No longer would she have to put up with his lies. And yet, she would miss him dearly. He was her only friend.

The next day the Master walked out with her once more to tend to the horses. He again helped guide her through the things that needed to be done but they went much faster the second day. Master Ruddick let her stay out a short time after they finished the work so she could talk to the animals. The horses greatly appreciated her presence.

The third day he let her take the lead and everything went swimmingly. When she finished with the horses, he then told her she also needed to feed the chickens and the pigs. The chickens were easy to take care of in their penned in coop but the pigs she found rather disgusting. They smelled horrible, and they were a tad mean.

That night the Master welcomed a guest, and it was up to her to see to the woman's horse. She recognized the woman from the last dinner, who was surprised at the Girl being the one to take care of her horse.

"Well thank you, my dear," she said as the Girl held the horses bridle like the Master had shown her. "I do believe the sunlight agrees with you. What is your name again?"

The Girl eyes fell to the ground. "I don't have one, Mistress," she said softly.

"Truly? Well we must look into that one day, shan't we? My name is Celeste. And this is Vibrant." Celeste gently patted the side of the horse's head.

"That's a very pretty name," the Girl replied. "They are both very pretty."

"Well, aren't you sweet? Thank you. Vibrant is a spirited one, well suited to his name. But I'm sure you can tell that yourself." The woman glanced at Master Ruddick, who stood in the doorway, and turned back to the Girl. "Bed him down. I will be spending the night."

The Girl needed Dorinda's help to unsaddle the horse but in no time he was safe in his stall and munching on oats. The cook then had her gather some eggs before she needed to clean the dining room. Once that task was complete, Dorinda asked the Girl to help her in the kitchen. Again, something she'd never done before.

Once the meal was ready, she told the Girl to go into the library and inform the Master and his guest. Her slippered feet whisked upon the hardwood floor as she hastened down the hall. When she entered the library, she skidded to a halt. The Master and Mistress were standing quite close. Master Ruddick was holding Jasper's cage, and Mistress Celeste was gently waving her hands in the direction of the hare. There was little doubt that Mistress Celeste was also a priest of Chaos and she was doing something to Jasper.

"Yes," the priestess said to Master Ruddick, "the resonance is quite strong."

The Master simply nodded his head in reply.

"Dinner is ready, Master Ruddick," the Girl said hesitantly as she eyed the cage. She could feel Jasper trying to reach out to her but she steadfastly refused to let him in.

"I want you to help Dorinda with the service tonight," Master Ruddick told the Girl then sent her on her way.

The dinner was the oddest the Girl had ever witnessed. The entire time the Master and Mistress just stared into each other's eyes while they ate and talked. Sometimes they even fed each other. And no matter how much they ate the Girl felt a strong hunger roiling within both.

The Girl had difficulty sleeping that night. Something about the way Mistress Celeste looked at Jasper unnerved the Girl. She had a feeling that the Mistress was doing something to him when she had entered the library. Not that she really cared. But for several hours after she went to bed she thought she heard squealing and crying. She hoped they weren't hurting him. Again, not that she cared.

The following morning, with the help of the cook, she re-saddled the Mistress's horse. She walked Vibrant to the front door as Master Ruddick and Mistress Celeste came through.

"I will have my man come for him as soon as I get home," Mistress Celeste said to the Master before turning and taking the reins to her horse from the Girl.

"So, did Vibrant tell you any secrets?" the lovely priestess asked the Girl who shook her head no. The priestess smiled, cupped her hand under the Girl's chin and lifted her head slightly to look her in the eyes.

"Ruddick is right. You are a precious one." The priestess then leaned over and kissed the Girl on the forehead.

"It's a good thing I like Ruddick, or I'd try and steal you for myself."

As the woman rode away, the Girl turned to Master Ruddick. He wasn't happy about the Mistress's last comment or the kiss.

"Finish up your work then come back inside," he instructed her softly before turning and walking back into the manor.

It came to her as a bit of a surprise when she realized it was the first time she'd been left alone outside. But it didn't last long. Soon Dorinda came out and helped her with some of the more difficult work about the yard. The Girl might have believed Dorinda had come out merely to help, but she read Dorinda's emotions and knew the cook was on guard.

That evening a carriage arrived while the Girl was cleaning the foyer. A man quickly jumped out and made his way inside the manor. He returned a short time later with the Master. The man held a frantic Jasper in his cage. The hare had no idea what was going on and the Girl still refused to open up to him. But when the man left with her only friend, she was sick with guilt. She knew she'd never see him again, and she hadn't even said goodbye.

Three more days of the same routine and the Girl grew faster and faster with the work as she learned to love it. At the end of that third day she realized the Master had not come out with her at all. And neither had Dorinda. She was truly alone in the yard. She walked to the side of the manor and stared at the road that stretched into the unknown distance. She then turned her gaze on the woods surrounding the manor. Nothing was there to stop her from running. Only where would she go? She knew no one. She knew nothing of what lay beyond that yard and the Master looked after her. But did he really care for her? Jasper's last words still clung to her mind.

To the Master she was still just a thing to enjoy. The hunger always lingering there in his mind and it disgusted her. The previous night he again came to her chamber and had his way with her. With each passing day his hunger grew stronger—his guilt was nearly gone. She belonged to him as simple as that.

She took one last long look at the road and walked toward the manor. She glanced up and saw Master Ruddick watching her through the upstairs window, smiling. She knew no matter how free she may feel, he would always watch her.

That night, as she drifted asleep, Master Ruddick entered her room. He stared at her for a moment, then said, "You are, and always will be, mine. Remember that." He smiled and left.

That night she dreamt of a horrible, grasping monster... that loved her.

Sorrow's Heart   G. S. Scott

Chapter 10

Tears

"Master Ruddick said that you're not to deal with the outside work today," Dorinda told the Girl. "He said to just do the foyer and the dining room as he is having another group of guests this evening."

The Girl felt crestfallen. She truly looked forward to working with the horses, particularly as it seemed like it would be a wonderful day outside. And if the Master was having another dinner like the last one, then she needed to appear her best. The Master most likely wanted to show her off some more.

As she worked on polishing the tables in the foyer she saw Kenneth rushing back and forth. With all the work she'd been doing outside she hadn't seen him in several days. He seemed a bit frazzled to the Girl, but then again the snotty young man always seemed a bit twitchy.

Once finished with the dining room she went to see the cook about a bath. If she was to look her best she knew she would need one. Once Dorinda scrubbed her body and washed her hair, she headed up to her chambers to dry, get dressed, and brush her hair. She felt a bit on edge herself. She noticed Dorinda also felt on edge as she bathed her. The Girl didn't know what it meant, but it had her worried.

As she turned the corner of the hall to go to her room, she saw the Master waiting there. "Hello, my precious. Are you going to go get dressed?" When she nodded he smiled. "Wonderful. I want you to wear your green dress today and I've had Dorinda lay out some stockings and a nice pair of new shoes for you. I want you to look resplendent this evening."

"I'm sorry, Master, what is 'respen'—"

"Just go do as I told you," he cut her off with a soft but firm tone. As he walked away, he stopped a moment and looked back. "Remember, I said the green one. It will go wonderfully with your eyes." His smile was warm yet predatory.

She hastened to her room and threw off her work dress. Racing to her wash table, she filled the bowl with the pitcher of water she placed there earlier. She took her tooth stick, dampened it, and dipped it in some salt to brush her teeth, something she did almost every day at the insistence of the Master.

She then towel dried her hair which took some time as it lay halfway down her back now. Once dry she brushed it one hundred times, just like Dorinda taught her. She then pulled out the green dress the Master wanted. The pleated dress was rather short, hanging only halfway to her knees. It tied in the front but only up as far as the center of her chest. She wore it only once before when the Master first bought it for her.

She went to the bed and got the shoes and stockings the Master spoke of. The bright white stockings came up to her knees where she tied them off with a silken tie string. Then she put on the polished black shoes, each with a silver buckle. She'd worn nothing like them before and they felt uncomfortable to her. She much preferred her slippers.

After walking back to her stand, she brushed her hair again to straighten it then tied it off in back with the green silk tie that came with the dress. She observed herself in the mirror. She didn't know what to think. She looked odd, like she was trying to show off too much.

"That's the idea," said a voice that bloomed into her mind.

After a moment she realized she'd heard the wolf in the basement which astonished her. She'd not seen it in some time and suddenly there he was, like he stood in the same room.

"What do you want?" she asked tartly out loud.

"Nothing," it replied. "You were wondering why he wanted you to look that way so I told you."

"How would you know what I look like?" she questioned.

"Because you are looking at yourself in the mirror," he replied mirthfully.

"You can see through my eyes?" she said, astonished. "When could you start doing that?"

"I've always been able to." The wolf's mirth then vanished becoming quite serious. "I've been watching you from the moment I arrived."

"How can I hear you so well yet I can't even see you?"

"You don't want that answer."

"What do you mean by that?" she asked, but the wolf did not reply. "What did you mean?" Even though she had yelled, the wolf again went silent. She stomped her foot in frustration.

At midafternoon, the Master's guests started to arrive, and the Girl heard Kenneth greet them at the door before escorting them to the library. Initially the Girl helped Dorinda with the food serving, but once the preliminary course ended, the Master told her to stay at his side.

The Girl stared at the Master's guests. She recognized the first, Mistress Celeste. She wore a bright red dress that tightly hugged her form and was cut as low as the Girl's, but then Mistress Celeste displayed a fair amount of bosom. The priestess radiated pride mixed with aggressiveness. And every time she glanced at the Girl she held a hunger. It differed as to when the Master looked at her. The priestess's hunger was more covetous, as though she saw something she wanted more than anything else in the world.

Next to Mistress Celeste sat a heavy set bald man in blue robes. He held an ever- present slight grin, as though he knew a secret no one else knew. She didn't like him, particularly when he looked at her. Each time he did his smile grew wider and even more knowing.

Across from the bald man slumped a tall, skinny man in a gray shirt and bright red breeches. He had a sour expression on his dark tanned, narrow face framed by dark, wild hair hanging to his shoulders. And atop his head he wore a silly looking, tall cone-shaped hat.

Next to the man in the silly hat perched a woman, much older than Mistress Celeste, her long and gray hair held in a net at the back of her head. Her face, creased and wrinkled, held a sour expression as well. She ran her hands down her sky blue dress every time she looked at Mistress Celeste, filled with envy.

They talked about people and things in the outside world she knew nothing about. They talked about a man named Heartless and lands filled with dead people and prisons. They spoke of political moves by someone called Hannibal, and how he berated someone named Flint for being too "persistent" in still chasing those that missed the cleansing. She had to admit it sounded odd for a priest to be so worried about cleanliness.

The Girl fidgeted at Master Ruddick's side. She worried as to her reason for being there and why they seemed to be all but ignoring her. Regardless, she did her best to calm herself. The Master had her there for a reason and she would eventually find out.

Her mind drifted, and she thought about many things—how the horses fared, the way the wind caressed her skin whenever she was allowed outside, and the unnecessary shortness of her dress, but mostly she wondered why the wolf in the basement suddenly spoke to her for no apparent reason.

Mostly, Master Ruddick said nothing. He just watched his guests as they interacted. The Girl came out of her introspection when the Master spoke up, interrupting his guests conversation.

"What were you able to find out about the hare, Celeste?" Master Ruddick asked.

"It was quite fascinating," she replied after taking a drink of her wine. "It appeared to have been Tebutaran in nature and had strong connections to the True Tree. Spirit's residue was quite strong in it. Frankly, I don't know if I've ever seen higher."

"What do you mean 'was'?" the Girl blurted out.

"It means just what you think it does, my dear," the Mistress smiled and replied blithely. "How else am I supposed to filter its essence?"

"You mean Jasper's dead?" Her heart sank, filled with horror.

"You didn't want him anymore," was the woman's response.

"You did say it did nothing but lie to you, my precious," Master Ruddick interjected. "I'd think you would be happy about it." His smile may have been sweet, but she felt the wickedness behind it.

"But he was my best friend," she said, her voice slightly cracking as she fought back her tears. "He taught me so much. He taught me words I never knew before!"

"Please tell me you are not saying that the child could communicate with a rabbit?" said the man in the tall, silly hat. "Constantine told me that you were trying to convince him of that at your last dinner. The idea is absolutely preposterous."

"The child believes she can," replied the bald man in blue.

"Zaneda is the most amazing person in the world in the matters of the mind, you know," Master Ruddick said to the man in the silly hat.

"I thank you, Ruddick, for the compliment." The bald man gave a slight nod. "I am good, it is true, but I'm hardly the best. I'm no Koren Laylear."

"I understand," Master Ruddick replied. "But your specialty is in the reading of one's thoughts, is it not?"

"Amongst other things, yes," the bald man stated with a smile.

"Tell our dubious friend here what is in the mind of my precious little one," the Master instructed.

The bald man nodded and looked at the Girl. "The child can read people's emotions. She's reading us at this very moment. Plus, she is despondent over the loss of her friend. She is doing her best not to cry, something she had promised herself she would never do." His face quirked into a small smile. "But she is also rebellious and quite good at subconsciously hiding it. I could do something about that if you like. I have worked with her before."

The comment shocked the Girl. She'd no memory of ever seeing the bald man.

"When was this?" Mistress Celeste asked, her eyes passing from the Girl to the bald man and back again.

"Back when Ruddick acquired her," he replied. "She was quite fragile back then. We felt she needed something to give her strength, an anchor of some kind."

"Truly?" inquired the man in the funny hat. "I'm surprised you cared, the way you go through children."

"She came at considerable expense," Master Ruddick told him. "She wasn't just some guttersnipe picked up at random."

"Indeed," the bald man said. "So, as I was saying, we felt she needed something. I sold our dear Rudy one of my lesser boys. He was to be one of my houseboys but proved to be an utter failure. Therefore, I sold him to Ruddick and implanted the idea into both of them that they were brother and sister. I'd say it worked quite well considering our young lady here is shocked upon only now finding out the truth."

The Girl was more than shocked, it floored her. Rosh wasn't her brother? She'd always wondered, but she played it off as a flight of fancy whenever she was angry with him. What else had the bald priest done to her in the past?

The bald man stared at her with a knowing smile. "As I was saying, Rudy. She's acquired quite a stubborn streak. Do you want me to fix that?"

"Another time, perhaps," the Master said sourly. "What else is going on in her mind?"

"Well, she thinks that Dimitri's hat is silly. Nearly as much as I do," he remarked with a smile then paused. "Interesting. There is something else in her mind. Along with her own thoughts I can also sense those of something else, something… animalistic. I'm guessing it is some kind of canine but the thoughts are subtle. I do believe it is listening to us."

"The wolf in the basement?" Master Ruddick seemed surprised. "Anything else?" he pressed.

"Yes. I can sense something else there as well," the priest muttered with a slight shake of the head. "Something quite vast. But I can tell nothing more about it than that."

His eyebrows raised slightly. "It's gone! Fascinating. The girl is a wonder on so many levels."

"As I told you." Master Ruddick smiled at the man in the silly hat.

"That is amazing," the man in the silly hat replied in wonder. "And you were able to imbue her with these wonderful gifts?"

The Master nodded.

"And yet I can now sense almost no residual flows in her, only Spirit," Mistress Celeste added. "Why do you think that is?"

"I do not know," he answered. "I was hoping you might help with that. You are the most renowned in matters of Spirit."

"Let us see her speak to the wolf. Perhaps I will be able to detect something," she said to the Master. "If you don't mind that is?"

"Not at all. I didn't even know that she could converse with it," he said softly. "I thought it nothing more than a common wolf."

The Girl sensed his displeasure.

They made their way into the basement with the Girl reluctantly in the lead. The wolf, sitting upon its haunches, watched them enter one at a time. It wasn't perturbed in the slightest. It just stared at them, measuring them with its eyes.

"Go on, my dear," Mistress Celeste coaxed her.

She turned to Master Ruddick, who gave a nod, and then to the wolf. "What's your name?" she asked. But the wolf refused to answer. She glanced nervously at the bald man. She couldn't lie and just say it never happened, he would know. His smile was proof. "Come on, what's your name? Why won't you talk to me? You talked to me this afternoon so why not now?" She then swallowed hard. "They don't want to harm you, they just want to see that I can do it."

"Lies don't become you, little cub," it said.

"She did it," exclaimed the bald man. "I could hear it in her mind. The wolf knew she was lying as well. Fascinating! Such intellect from a simple animal."

"It is hardly simple," Mistress Celeste remarked with a smile.

"Well," the man in the silly hat said, "this calls for a toast! We must congratulate our esteemed Ruddick. What he has done is spectacular!"

"Let us withdraw back to the dining room then," Master Ruddick declared, sweeping his hand toward the stairs.

"You are to stay here, my sweet," he said to her. "I want you to find out all you can about your new wolf friend here. I believe there is much we can learn from him."

The Girl did not like the feelings she received from the Master. She knew the wolf would soon be headed to Mistress Celeste's like Jasper had. She sat and stared despondently at the wolf. She knew what was coming and she could do nothing about it. She had no choice in the matter.

"Vir," the wolf said solemnly.

"What?" she asked, confused.

"You asked earlier so I'm telling you. My name is Vir."

"But why wouldn't you say so earlier? You made me look foolish," she said, pouting.

"Because I didn't want the priest to know my name," he replied with a grin.

"But, why?"

"Because it's none of his business," he answered matter-of-factly. "I don't want some nosy Chaos priest walking around knowing my name." He then added, "Oh, and you do have a choice."

"What are you talking about?" she asked with a shake of her head. "You're so confusing!"

"You do have a choice as to what to do, my little cub. We all have choices. Some have more than others, true, but everyone has choices, nonetheless." Vir lay down and placed his head upon his paws.

"But what can I do?"

"That is up to you, little one. You are strong. Far stronger than you know. And you're very clever. They all see it, it's why they are so fascinated with you."

"I fascinate them because the Master turned me into a freak," she harrumphed. "That and they stare at me like they all want to eat me."

"Yes, there is that. Most human adults are not like that, from what I understand, but for some reason the priests of Chaos have turned particularly dark as of late. To most, you are just a young girl about to flower into womanhood. But to those of power, those that are strong in the ways of the Lord of Chaos, they only see something to use to satisfy all their desires and urges." He shook his head in disgust.

"What do I do, Vir?" she quietly begged.

"You know what to do, sweetling," he stated.

She stared at him, filled with doubt, then slowly got to her feet and went to see if anyone was on the stairs. With no one there she crept back and knelt before the cage door. She did know what to do. She'd seen the Master do it many times with the animal cages. She pulled up the pin and undid the latch on Vir's door and swung it open.

"The Master will kill me for this," she whispered.

"Not if you don't want him to," Vir replied. "Now you run along. I will wait till nightfall and then make my escape." As she reached the bottom of the steps he added, "Remember, little cub, you always have a choice."

She nodded, albeit doubtfully, and went to bed. Maybe the Master would think one of the others had freed Vir. She took off her shoes, mounted the stairs, and quickly made her way to and through the kitchen. As she walked down the hall, she still heard the Master and his company talking in the dining room, so she sneaked by. She made it to the top of the stairs without seeing Kenneth or Dorinda, for which she was grateful. She rushed to her room, threw off her clothes, and climbed into bed. As she fell asleep, she prayed the Master would never find out who freed Vir.

"How dare you try and take what is mine!" Master Ruddick shouted, waking her up. "That wolf was mine! This house is mine! You are mine! I would have thought you had learned that long ago. It would appear you need to be reminded."

He stood in the doorway, holding a bottle of brandy. He took a sip then threw the bottle against the wall, shattering it. He quietly walked to her bedside and with his powers threw her bed sheets to the floor.

She quivered in terror.

"I'm done being gentle with you," he snapped as he climbed onto the bed. With a snarl he slapped her hard across the face, causing her to scream in pain. Grabbing her legs, he forced them open. As he undid the drawstring on his breeches, the Girl closes her eyes and tried to picture herself somewhere else. Anywhere else.

"Why do you do this, little one?" Vir's voice boomed strong in her mind. "There is more to life than this."

"But what can I do?" she pleaded.

"You learn that I own you. You learn that you do everything I want and I will do anything I want to you!" the Master shouted as he took her.

She did not hear Master Ruddick, his painful assault washed through her. She only heard Vir.

"Choose," Vir said somberly. "Choose now."

The pain of her Master's—No! The priest's thrusts lit a fire deep within her. It burned hotter and hotter until it exploded.

She chose.

"No!" she screamed, digging her fingernails into the horrible priest's face, gouging his cheeks and one of his eyes.

The man pulled back with a howl. "How dare you!" He held a hand to his bleeding face. "You will pay for that!" He raised his other hand, and it glowed. A multicolored ball of gelatinous ooze filled it. "I think I'll take your legs first," he said with a snarl. "I really don't need those."

The priest did not see the shadow form behind him.

Vir lunged and sunk his teeth into Ruddick's throat. With a shake, he tore it out. Sprays of hot blood drenched the Girl's face. She crawled away as the priest fell onto the bed, clasping at his ruined throat. He gurgled and thrashed and then went silent. Forever.

Vir stood on the bed over the worthless priest's body. The Girl flung herself at him and hugged him fiercely around the neck. "Thank you," she panted, still trembling. "Thank you! Thank you! Thank you!"

"Come, little one, we must leave."

Now that the priest was dead his mystic light died with him, leaving the room nearly pitch black. With the help of Vir, the Girl got up, and using the dress she wore at the dinner, wiped the priest's blood off as best she could.

After dressing in her simplest dress and slippers, they crept out into the hall and made for the backdoor. The Girl insisted they release all the animals from the basement. They had been imprisoned long enough.

She told the animals to be as quiet as they could so as not to alert Kenneth or the cook. But in truth she didn't care if anyone heard. Vir would dispatch Kenneth as he had the priest. And if they came upon Dorinda... well, the Girl hoped the cook could be reasoned with.

She urged all to silence as she ushered them all up the stairs and out the back kitchen door. As they walked out onto the moonlit stable yard she asked Vir, "How did you ever get caught in the first place?"

"I let them take me."

"What?" she said, shocked. "Why would you do that?"

"Because Mother asked me to," he replied.

"Don't you dare start with that!"

But Vir went on anyway. "It is the truth. Search my thoughts and you will see. The Mother foresees something great in you. And the moment you gained her consciousness she sent me to try and convince you to leave this place."

The Girl shook her head in anger. It couldn't be true, it just couldn't! Because if it was, then Jasper...

"He was telling you the truth," Vir said solemnly. "I am sorry. But you must not blame yourself. You did not know that they would kill him."

His heartfelt words were of little solace. She was responsible! She, a nameless girl who Jasper had only tried to be nice to and teach, caused his death.

"Again, you are not responsible, little one. And you are not nameless," Vir said with a shake of his head.

The Girl's brows furrowed. "Yes I am. I have no name, I never have."

"Of course you have a name," Vir said with a grin. "And I don't mean one of the epithets the priest used for you."

"Epa-what?"

"Nickname. The things he called you," Vir explained. "You have a real name. Tell me it, please?"

"I don't remember," she answered stubbornly.

"Yes you do," Vir soothed. "I can see it in the back of your mind. It's all right. You can say it."

She didn't want to. It was hard to remember that far back, and it made her angry because it was given to her by her mother, the mother that simply threw her away.

"It was not like that," Vir said softly. "Here, I will help you."

She felt Vir push into her mind. He guided and helped her think about her life so long ago. She saw that her mother did indeed give her a name. Why would she do such a thing if she really didn't want her? And if her mother truly didn't want her why could she remember her mother calling out her name? Why was her mother crying and calling out her name as the priest tore the Girl from her arms? Crying out the very name she chose to forget.

The Girl felt her throat tighten.

"You can do it, little cub," Vir prodded softly. "I know it hurts but you must do it. It's the only way to let it go and heal."

The Girl fought and fought but the tears formed in her eyes. She trembled and there was nothing she could do about it. She finally did what she promised herself she never would. She cried.

Tears streamed down her face as she buried it into Vir's fur. "Daylin," she cried out. "My name is Daylin!" She sobbed and clung to Vir with trembling arms.

Daylin didn't know how long she stood there, crying into Vir's wonderful fur. But the entire time she felt her friend's pride in her, the pride he felt in her strength and courage. It shone like the sun.

"That is a wonderful name, my little cub," he said after a while. "Daylin. Daylin with a dragon in her veins. Yes, that is your true name, my little cub. You are Daylin Dragonvein."

"I like that," Daylin sniffled as she wiped away her tears. A thought sprung into her mind. "We have to let the horses go as well."

She sprinted to the stables. Daylin quickly released Wind, telling him he was free to run wherever and whenever he wanted. She then went to Casandra's stall and opened it. Slowly walking in, she placed the stool next to the sad horse and stood upon it so she looked her in the eyes.

"I remember now," Daylin murmured with a sad smile. "I remember where I heard your name."

She cried again as she hugged the horse about the neck. "I forgive you, Mother." She sobbed, thinking about the woman who bore her, who truly loved her until the moment the priest killed her trying to protect her child—the woman for whom Daylin named the horse. "I love you, Mother, and I always will."

After she freed the horses, Daylin stood and looked down the lane leading away from the manor. She didn't know what lay down that lane, and she didn't care. That was not her world.

She took hold of Vir's fur and they headed off into the woods, under the beautiful starlit sky, away from the lane and the manor and the life she had there. She was no longer afraid. Daylin Dragonvein had a family once more and no one would ever imprison her again.

"Let them try," she growled with a flash of her teeth. "We'll rip out their throats."

Acknowledgements:

I wish to thank Randy Pearson for inspiring me to go through with this.

I wish to thank my many friends at home, Tommy, Stacy, Laurie, William, and Stephanie, for their support; as well as those on WriteOn for their help in the proofreading.

I wish to thank Colleen Nye for her continued support.

I also wish to thank my folks, Jerry and Barb for your years of love and support, and Dean Hauck at the Michigan News agency in Kalamazoo, Mi.

Lastly, and most certainly not least, I want to thank my Angel Eyes, Sarah Hauck. I couldn't have done it without you.

Sorrow's Heart   G.S. Scott

About The Author:

G. S. Scott is a published author who works at a civil engineering firm in Lansing, Michigan. He enjoys writing all types of fantasy stories and poetry. He is active in local writing groups and is an avid gamer. He enjoys local theater with his playwright wife, Sarah. They share their home with her wonderful cat and their overenthusiastic dog.

Sorrow's Heart   G.S. Scott

Author links:

http://www.g-s-scott.com/

https://www.facebook.com/GregorySScott/

https://www.goodreads.com/author/show/14213028.G_S_Scott

https://twitter.com/GregorySScott

Sorrow's Heart   G.S. Scott

Also by G.S. Scott:

The True Tree Chronicles: Cleansed

Keep watch for more by G.S. Scott in:

The True Tree Chronicles: Chaos Reigns: The Hand of God

Made in the USA
Columbia, SC
28 August 2018